REQUESTED TRILOGY

PART ONE

don't

say

a

word

by Sabre Rose

For more information about the author visit:

www.sabreroseauthor.com

ISBN: 9781791844882

Kneel. Submit. Obey.

I have been taken by a man unknown to me.

But he is not the one who holds me captive.

Not whose voice commands me.

Who watches me with a storm raging in ocean-blue eyes.

It is my captor who knows every inch of my body.

Who trains me for another man to ruin.

But I am not his.

I belong to my requestor.

Whoever he is . . .

This story contains dark scenes of a sexual nature.
Reader discretion is advised.

"I like beautiful melodies telling me terrible things."

- Tom Waits

CHAPTER ONE

REQUESTOR

The bar is disgusting. The fluorescent bulbs create a strange buzzing sound that reminds me of flies gathered around death. The wallpaper is torn and mold clings in patches to the ceiling. The people are loud and garish, throwing beer down their throats as though their lives depend on it. Maybe they do. Maybe this is all they can hope to amount to. They repulse me.

But then the lights dim and she steps onto the stage. A spotlight shines and she blinks, holding up her hand to shield her eyes from the glare. She laughs nervously, a sweet sound, one filled with such innocence, and takes a seat on the stool in front of the microphone.

She gives a small wave but doesn't say her name. I suppose in a town as small as this, everyone already knows it. Her cheeks burn when someone lets out a whoop and she runs her tongue over soft pink lips. Biteable lips.

My blood spikes and hums, lighting a fire in my veins and

electrifying my thoughts. I hadn't taken much notice of her before. Mistakenly, I thought she blended in with the rest of the trash around here. Small town people with small-town minds. But when the music starts and she closes her eyes, the world stills. Beyond the halo of light that surrounds her, nothing else exists.

She is exquisite in her beauty. Dark hair frames a pale face with lips that are full and soft and plump. She wears a pink dress that drapes over her figure, just hinting at her curves, but the neckline is low, dipping between the swells of her breasts and giving me a taste of her perfection.

And then she starts to sing. The halo of light expands, encasing me in its warmth, leaving nothing but our two souls in this world. My heart races. Her voice haunts me, slicing into my soul. Never before have I heard such soulful beauty. From the first note, her voice is flawless. Perfect.

But she knows none of the torment that creates music. From the innocence in her voice, I know she has not felt the affliction of love, has not suffered the misery of pain. If she had, her voice would be beyond perfection. It would be raw, her throat torn open, ragged with passion spilling like blood from an open wound. It would call out, beckoning me to drown in her as though she is a siren from the depths.

And that's when I know. She will be mine. And I will show her the world she is innocent of.

The humming of my blood grows louder. I want to touch. I want to inhale. I want to taste.

A girl bumps into me, knocking me back to reality and allowing the dirtiness of the world to seep back in. Anger flashes. A vision of grabbing her by the hair and yanking her head down to connect with my knee bursts like lightning through my mind. I would strike with enough force that her body would slump to the ground, leaving the halo of light that surrounds my songbird and me.

But instead I smile, looking over to her with what most people would decipher as warmth.

"Are you okay?" I ask.

It takes practice to control the strain in my voice, hiding the monster within. She smiles and holds up her glass as some sort of answer, stumbling a little and spilling beer onto the already stained carpet.

"You having fun?" she asks.

I deceive her with another smile, adding a wink for extra effect and she raises her glass again, pushing her body against mine in some infantile attempt at seduction. She's a pretty girl. A way to pass the time, but she's not the one I want. Not the one that speaks to my soul.

Turning my attention back to my songbird, the imbeciles around me carry on with their feeble lives, unable to hear the purity in her voice. Their laughter grates against my thoughts and I am unable to get lost in her. Their brutish behavior should not be allowed. She doesn't belong with them.

But sometimes the shadows of this world hide the most beautiful things. They sit in dark corners, their beauty undiscovered and their talents unseen. There are some who would take this beauty and shine a light on it for all the world to see. They would hold them in the glare of the spotlight until their beauty fades and their talents are wasted on those who are incapable of showing appreciation.

My father warned me of those people. The ones who allow beauty to become tarnished. He taught me to value the pretty things of this world and keep them safe. Protect them from the bright and garish lights. Keep them in the shadows so their beauty does not fade.

My father is a collector. He taught me the value of capturing beauty. But he missed something. He was obsessed with the vessel and unable to see that talent and passion and pain combined make something more than beauty. Something that seeps into the blood and feeds the soul.

My father's collection is lacking. It's time to start my own.

mia

CHAPTER TWO

MIA

Panic. My body feels it first. The swell of nausea in the pit of my stomach. The sense of dread. The tingling sensation of terror.

And then comes the thud of my heart. It's rapid, beating against my chest like a caged wild animal. It's all I can hear. It drowns out my other senses. Nothing but the pulse of my blood and the echo of my heart.

Sweat is next. Cold. Trembling. The kind that prickles over my skin, leaving trails of raised hairs and goosebumps.

Darkness crushes me. It is endless. My eyelids brush against rough material. I am blindfolded and for that I am grateful. Because if not for the movement of my eyelids against the material, I would have thought myself dead. It doesn't matter that my heart pounds in my chest or that my skin dances with dread, those things can be imagined. They could be my mind playing tricks. But the feel of that material and the tightness of the twist which holds it in place are real.

The floor is cold and hard, smooth like polished concrete.

My foot twitches and pain shoots through my leg with the stiffness of the movement.

Awareness creeps over me. I am kneeling on the floor, tilted to the side, resting on one hip. My back aches. My stomach aches. My head pounds. My hands are tied. No. They are chained. The rungs of metal are cold and hard as they dig into my flesh.

I wiggle my fingers. Nothing. My arms are dead. All the blood has drained from them as they hang above my head, enough to allow a bend at my elbows, enough to allow my head to rest against my forearms.

I test my restraints. The chains clank as they jostle together. I can move my hands up, from side to side, but I cannot pull them down. My left shoulder hurts more than my right. It is pressed to a wall that reflects the coldness and smoothness of the floor.

All parts of my body ache. It is a dull, deep ache. The type that has settled into my bones, stiff from sitting in the same position for however long I have been here.

Trying to sort through my thoughts is like wading through fog. Memories are there but I can't recall them. The cloud that has settled in my brain hides them from me. Maybe that is why I'm not screaming, not crying. Although my body drips with panic and dread, my mind is blank. And that terrifies me most of all.

I have no idea where I am, or why I'm here.

Wincing, I twist my body so I can sit on my backside, my

back pressed to the wall, my hands hanging at approximately the same level as my forehead. I stretch out my legs, push my feet over the smooth surface and wiggle my toes. Painful tingles of pins and needles torment my feet. I long to reach down and rub them. Push my fingers into the webbing of my toes for relief. Stretch the tendons. Massage the sensation away.

Then I laugh. It is just a small bubble of sound, but it escapes my lips and falls into the empty space. I am tied— no—chained. I have no idea how I got here, why I am here, and yet, I am worried about the pins and needles in my feet.

I laugh again. But it is a splutter this time. A series of foamy bubbles at the back of my throat that eventually turn to tears.

And then I sob.

I scream.

I jerk on my chains.

I kick out across the floor.

I bang my head against the wall.

But none of it makes any difference. No one comes to my rescue.

The silence is deafening. Only my own voice echoes around the small space. At least, I think it must be small. It sounds small. It sounds as though I am trapped, that no one can hear me because my screams reverberate off the walls until I'm no longer sure if I am still screaming or if I am just left with the echo.

I scream for hours. For minutes. Or maybe for seconds. My throat is raw. There is something warm and damp running down my arms but I no longer feel pain. My arms don't ache. My shoulders, neck, stomach, and legs no longer exist. I am nothing but a pile of flesh and bones leaning against a wall.

But the fog that drapes over my mind like a blanket is beginning to lift. I still don't know anything, no answers as to where I am, why I am here, but little connections begin to form. I imagine them as sparks, linking the patterns of my brain. So I sit silent and still, waiting for them to make sense. Waiting for them to give me the answers I'm looking for.

There is this part, the smallest part of me that hopes, or rather dreams, that this is some sick practical joke. That a door will clank open and the blindfold will be ripped from my eyes. I would blink, stunned by the sudden brightness, and people would shout 'surprise'. But the ache in my muscles tells me I have been here for too long. And the sensibility of my brain tells me that no one I know would be that cruel.

But I long for it. For some sort of sickness in one of my friends that might lead to them thinking a practical joke like that would be funny.

And then I hear it. The beep of a keypad, the hushed opening of a door, the feel of slightly warmer air hitting my skin.

"Hello?" I say. It isn't a scream or a cry. It's just one word, usually meant as a greeting and followed by a smile.

Silence.

"Hello?" I try again, this time louder. More desperate. "Is someone there?" My voice catches, a plea tearing my throat.

There is someone in the room. Whereas before I felt coldness and emptiness, now there is a presence. A dark presence.

"Hello? If you're there, if someone is there, please answer me."

Only silence.

I can smell them. Their scent is musky. A man's cologne mixed with wood and dirt.

"I know you're there." I try a different tack. One that doesn't show my fear, that doesn't have me cowering in the corner. I move to sit on my knees, ears scanning the room for a hint of sound that will betray his position.

There is a hitch of breath so quiet, so faint, that had my ears not been straining for a glimpse of sound, I would have missed it.

"I can hear you," I whisper. "I know you're there."

Footsteps. Quiet. Padded. As though the feet are bare. I jerk my head in various directions, trying to pinpoint the steps.

And then I feel the heat of him and I push myself against the wall, scrambling to my feet, certain he is close, certain he is going to touch me.

He doesn't.

His breath is hot and heavy. I can feel the heat of his body only inches away from mine. I begin to tremble again, so much so that the chains rattle.

"What do you want?" I ask the darkness.

No reply.

"Who are you?"

His heat dissipates and I am left cold.

"Hello?" I call out. "Are you still there?"

I can hear nothing but the sound of my own breath. It is quick and shallow. Panicked. Now that I'm standing with my arms lowered, the blood rushes back painfully. I clutch my left forearm with my right hand, rubbing back and forth, willing the pain to subside.

"Are you still there?" I ask again. Only this time my voice breaks. "Please?" I plead. "Please talk to me."

I am begging with my captor, whoever he is. He hasn't laid a finger on me, he hasn't uttered a word and yet, already I am begging.

"Just tell me why I'm here. Tell me what you are going to do with me." I don't know why I ask this. It isn't as though the knowledge of what is happening would lessen my terror.

I swallow painfully. My screaming has left my throat torn and my tears have left it tight and constricted. A whistle of air is the only thing to escape.

There is a clang above me. A mechanical sound that whirrs into life. And then the chains around my wrists tighten, lifting my arms higher into the air.

"No!" I shout, surprised by the force of my own voice. I thought it had gone. "No, no, no." I twist against my restraints, creating a fresh trickle of blood that trails down my arm. "Please," I beg, as though it will make a difference, as though something can appeal to the darkness that surrounds me.

Up and up the chains lift until I am stretched on my tiptoes, my body protesting at being stretched to its full length.

I hang my head, uncontrollable sobs wrenched from me as I struggle to maintain balance on the tips of my toes. Maybe that's why I don't hear the footsteps as they approach. Maybe that's why I am startled when something brushes against me.

A finger runs down my arm with skin that is calloused and rough. My sobs stop, getting caught in my chest along with my breath. The finger trails down my arm slowly, pulling a line of blood, drawing on my skin like he is enjoying the torment he knows his touch inflicts. The torment of the unknown.

His touch doesn't burn so much once it is shielded by the material of my sleeve. He runs it over my armpit and down my side until it trips over the waistband of my jeans. Then it just stays there, hooked for a second, or maybe it's a moment disguised as an eternity. When the movement starts again, creeping along my waistband, slipping closer and closer to the buttons of my jeans, I scream.

I scream loud and long and hope I shatter his eardrums. His finger leaves abruptly so I stop screaming, but when it comes back to sear my skin, I scream again. With all my strength, I scream until I imagine my vocal cords snapping and I am wrenched into silence. Only, it isn't the snap of my vocal cords that silences me, it is the loss of air as firm hands shove me against the wall, lifting my feet from the ground. Something presses against my throat. His arm? I can't concentrate on what it feels like because it cuts off all the air to my lungs. I gasp, pressed against the wall. I flail my feet, a surge of triumph rising when one connects with what I can only assume is the shin of his leg and a grunt of air is expelled. The pressure against my throat lessens and I swing back, my toes searching for the ground.

But he is still there. I can feel his eyes on me.

He leaves me dangling for a few moments and I hope he will give up and leave me alone, even if that means dangling from the ceiling, wrists in chains and feet constantly searching for the security of the floor. It's better than being here with him, having his hands run over my body, one step away from doing things I don't want to think about.

Then my feet are swung from the ground, his hand is at my neck and I am pressed against the wall again. He is quick this time. Quick and rough. My shirt is ripped open and buttons fall to the floor like rain. Coldness presses against me and I hear a slice as my bra is removed. His hand falls from my neck and I swing like a pendulum, my toes frantically grabbing at the floor. I scream again but it doesn't matter. His hands claw at my jeans, wrestling them over my hips. I flail again and this time my knee connects with a sharp part of him, but he doesn't stop. He keeps tearing at my clothes until they are gone and I am left naked and dangling.

The chains rattle with my trembling. But I don't scream this time. By now I know there is no point. If anyone else was here, they would have come to help by now. Either that, or they are in on it too.

And one dose of evil is enough.

I expect his hands to come back. I expected them to brush against my skin and take what they desire. But the only thing that greets me is the clunk of the chain as it starts to lower.

The room grows colder and darker. Colder and darker than it was when he was present. That's how I know I am alone.

That's how I know he is gone.

For now.

CHAPTER THREE

MIA

My body jerks. It is only then I realize I must have fallen
asleep. I didn't think it was possible. But there's something
heavy that keeps dragging me back to that oblivion.
Surrounded by silence and darkness, time has become a
meaningless concept. I don't know how long I've been here.
It must be hours. But how many, I don't know. There is
nothing to measure the time and time doesn't exist if it
cannot be measured.

No light.

No sound.

Nothing.

My body is numb. It hurts to move. Every time I attempt
to shuffle across the cold floor, or roll my shoulders, or try
to stretch out my legs, a sharp jolt of pain reminds me it is
pointless. My muscles and bones are nothing more than a
memory of my captivity.

I've given up yelling for help as there is no one here to
listen. I imagine myself in a room with a large wall of one-

way glass. Maybe I'm in some sort of social experiment to measure the levels of terror of people in captivity. Maybe they are watching me, scribbling notes, silently observing. Maybe someone took me in error. Any explanation other than the obvious.

I have been kidnapped.

Summoning what little strength I have left, I test the boundaries of my chains. They haven't changed. There is still a wall behind me, a floor below me. Nothing else I can decipher.

My thoughts remain thick as syrup, though some are pushing their way to the fore. Like saying goodbye to my mother. Walking to the front door, waving goodbye with her blowing a kiss like she always does. But I don't know if it's a memory of yesterday or a memory of two thousand yesterdays ago. I've said goodbye to her a million times over the years. A thousand times she's blown me a kiss. A thousand times she's watched out the window, frantically waving, a smile plastered on her face. A thousand times I hopped into my car and drove away.

So what memory was I recalling?

The last time I saw her, or one of the thousands of times before?

Was that my last memory before I was taken?

What happened next?

I push through the fog, trying to remember how I ended up here. Who put me here. But it is pointless. The harder I try, the harder I push, the thicker the fog gets.

I'm brought back to reality by the beeps of a keypad and the gush of air signaling the opening door. It's not a creak or a groan, more of a sigh.

It is him. I know this because of his scent. The same as before. Musk and wood and dirt. His footsteps are still padded. I can't feel the heat of him so I know he isn't close. My skin prickles. I wonder if he is watching me, if his eyes are roaming my naked flesh. Panic ignites and I push the thought from my mind.

"Hello?" I say.

He clears his throat. It's a deep sound and my head automatically twists in the direction it comes from.

"Hello?" I say again. Only this time it is more desperate.

"Don't say a word." His voice is a command.

"Please," I beg. "There's been a mistake. I—" But before I can finish a hand clamps to the back of my head and something soft is shoved in my mouth, muffling my startled scream. Further and further he forces the material until I can't make a sound. I can barely breathe as it pushes against the back of my throat and I gag. Tape is stretched across my mouth to hold it in.

"Don't say a word."

My tears can't fall; instead, they soak into the material covering my eyes. My screams can't echo; instead, they get lost in the material shoved in my mouth. So I stay still, pressed against the wall, waiting in terror for what will happen next.

Then I hear it, that same mechanical clunk of before, and the chains begin to rise. I struggle to get to my feet before I am dragged. My body cries out at the movement but the chains keep lifting until I find myself, once again, stretched on my toes, swaying to balance myself.

A whimper gets caught in my throat as he touches the skin below my right wrist. Just a single finger that slides slowly along my arm, the tip of it rough and calloused. It trails down my forearm and over the bump of my elbow. I resist the urge to cry as it slips lower, brushing over my armpit and just missing the swell of my breast. He stops when he reaches my hip and changes direction, drawing a line across my belly. And then he repeats the action in reverse, up the other side of my body.

I attempt to suck in air and material scratches the back of my throat. I gag again. I am suffocating and hyperventilating at the same time. My lungs scream as I retch over and over, desperate for anything to stop this nightmare.

"Breathe."

I barely hear the word as panic engulfs me.

"Breathe through your nose." His words are clipped and short, almost as though he's annoyed at my terror.

I'm trembling. The chains rattle. I struggle for balance.

"Through your nose," he repeats. "There is nothing blocking your nose. You are okay. You are safe. Just breathe."

If I wasn't so filled with fear, I might laugh. Safe. No part of me feels safe. But strangely enough, his voice brings some sense of comfort. No, that's not the right word. A sense of calm. My toes steady on the floor and I begin to breathe through my nose.

He waits, watching me. I can feel it as sure as I can feel my lungs filling with air. The chain lowers a little and my heels embrace the cold ground.

"Next time," he says, "don't say a word."

Then there is the hushed whisper of air as the door opens and closes, the keypad beeps and I am left alone again.

This time I don't have the luxury of sitting. He's lowered my chains so I can stand firmly on my feet, but my body is still stretched and my hands are high in the air above me. I am neither hot nor cold. I cannot feel the air around me nor can I feel the parts of my body. Everything has melded into a single lump of existence.

Nothing but panic and terror.

Possibilities of why I am here begin to race through my mind, elevating my panic to uncontrollable levels. Again, I struggle to find air and it is only the memory of his voice, instructing me to breathe through my nose that brings me down again.

"Breathe," I chant internally. "In. Out. In. Out."

Panic is not my friend. It will not help me.

I need to figure out why I'm here, so I turn back to my memories, determined to unravel the mystery. Mentally, I scroll through my life. My parents, safe at home in their red brick house. My best friend Roxy. The residents of my small town. Nothing out of place. Nothing different. Nothing that would land me here.

I've led a life of quiet innocence. I have no enemies, no jealous lovers or ex-boyfriends. I surround myself with a small circle of family and friends and live in a town where things like this simply don't happen. We only have one police station. One doctor. One church. Two bars. Everyone knows my name. I am Mia Cooper, daughter of Abigail and Samuel Cooper. They own the local bakery and I work there too. This must be the work of a stranger. An outsider.

There's an itch between my breasts. Something is tickling me. Not literally but it may as well be. It's driving me insane. I twist and turn against my restraints but it's no use. No matter what I do the itch is there. All other parts of my body are numb. Nothing else exists. Just me and the itch. And it is about to be my undoing. Not the chains that hold me, the darkness that surrounds me, my nakedness, the unknown. No.

It is an itch.

I let out a groan or a moan or a whimper that gets muffled by the gag. I try to scream. I fail.

Saliva pools under my tongue. I try thrashing my body but only succeed in creating fresh drips of blood that roll down my arms. At least I can feel them. At least they are something other than the itch.

And then another sensation starts. One that scares me more. I need to use the bathroom. Desperately.

I attempt to ignore the feeling by thinking of something else, anything else but the burning sensation of needing to relieve myself and it is only then that I remember walking away from the bar, the feeling of terror as a hand clamped over my mouth, the eyes gleaming in the darkness and a needle pressing into my skin. I remember fighting, scratching, clawing.

Then nothing.

Nothing until I woke here with panic prickling my skin.

The sharp pain of needing to go to the toilet twists in my lower gut. I cross my legs, pressing my thighs together and willing away the need. It doesn't help. The need only intensifies.

I don't want to pee myself. Somehow it seems more humiliating than being chained naked. But the need has increased to blindingly painful. Tears fall at the same time as relief floods my body and warmth trails down my legs. I draw in a giant sob, letting my head flop and my body relax, pulling against the restraints around my wrists.

Then the beeps sound again. The door opens. That rush of air. I whip my head in its direction, desperation and terror filling me.

And shame.

I am ashamed I pissed myself. Ashamed that a puddle of urine surrounds my feet even though I am facing a monster.

For who else could he be other than a monster, an animal?

His footsteps are clipped this time. He has shoes on. Panic swells my chest as he draws closer.

"Don't say a word." He tugs at the tape that runs halfway across my cheek.

I nod. Eagerly. Desperately.

"Speak and you will be punished. Do you understand?"

I nod again, anything to get the gag removed from my mouth, anything to breathe. The tape sticks to my skin as he slowly removes it. The material spills from my mouth. I swallow first, swallow the pool of saliva, swallow the tears at the back of my throat, and then I suck in gasps of air, allowing them to coat my lungs.

I hear the splash of water, the squeak of shoes as he kneels before me. I don't know how I know this. It's as though without my sight, my awareness has increased. But I long for vision. I long to be able to see the man before me and face my monster.

He is wringing out a cloth. I hear the splatter of water falling back into a bowl. I imagine hands, hard and calloused, twisting the material.

"I am going to clean you."

I nod again, the memory of being gagged too fresh to risk speaking. I flinch when he touches me.

"Don't," he warns. His voice isn't as filled with evil as I want it to be. It's deep and it's dark, it ignites terror within me but from fear of the unknown, not because of its tone.

I will myself to stay still as the warm cloth is pressed to my thigh again. Even though my eyes are bound shut, I close them tight as the cloth slides between my legs. I tense, but I resist the urge to squeeze them closed.

"Open," he instructs.

This time I shake my head. It's an involuntary movement. It happens before I can stop it. There is a whistle in the air and then something smacks against the back of my knees, buckling me. As I fall, the chain grips the flesh around my wrists. The pain of the lash was sharp and it stings, but it was the surprise of it that caused me to buckle.

"Open." His voice is firmer this time, allowing no disobedience.

I steady myself and shift my legs further apart. The cloth is pressed to my inner thigh and moves upward. A whimper escapes. A silent plea. Warmth brushes over my sex then falls down my legs, wiping me clean. The floor is next. The cloth makes a swooshing sound as it mops up the puddle of urine. Then there is the squeak of his shoes as he rises to his feet again.

"I am going to remove the blindfold."

I nod, my breath coming out in silent sobs.

Footsteps move behind me. His hands toy with the knot. The blindfold is removed but I keep my eyes shut, feeling the light invade even though they are closed. All I see is red. I don't know if I want to open them. Will sight increase my terror or lessen it? Do I want to see the man who has taken me?

I blink. Just once. Enough to allow the smallest amount of light to sting my eyes. I blink again, a few times in rapid succession. My vision is blurred. There is a square of light to my right and I twist away from it.

Slowly, I pluck up enough courage to open them fully. I can make out his figure sitting in a chair on the opposite side of the room.

I expected a monster but there is only a man.

Blue eyes stare back at me. No. They are green. Blue and green and gray, like the color of the ocean during a storm. He is sitting with his legs spread wide, elbows resting on his knees and hands clasped between them. I search him, scanning for familiarity, but I have never seen him before. He is a stranger.

"Who are you?" I ask.

Getting to his feet, he picks up the lash leaning against the wall. He stands behind me and I feel the sting of the whip again.

"Don't say a word," he growls. He walks around slowly, coming to a stop in front of me. "This is your command phrase. I will use it when I enter the room. You will obey my instructions. Do you understand?"

I nod again, my punishment bringing anger this time, not fear. I hope he can see it in my eyes. The defiance. The burst of insanity.

He stares back at me unflinchingly and I search those

ocean-eyes for a hint of humanity, a hint of regret or remorse, uncertainty or hesitation.

There is none.

His face is covered in a beard. Unkempt and messy. Deep furrows mark his forehead. His hair is thick and disheveled, long enough to tangle on the top yet it is clipped short around the sides.

I burn his image into my brain.

I will remember him in detail. One day, I will describe him to the police and I don't want to miss a thing. His clothing is unassuming, just a t-shirt, a jacket and jeans. His shoes look new, made of leather that squeaks when he walks.

His gaze is intense and I'm almost quivering with the need to look away. But I don't. If it were possible to square my shoulders, I would. Instead, I lift my chin and return his gaze. He blinks once and then turns and walks to where he sat before. There is a button on the wall and his finger hovers over it.

"I am going to unchain you now."

I nod once. A short acknowledgment that I won't try anything stupid. The chains lower and blood floods back down my veins painfully. I take the opportunity during his lack of attention to look around the room. For that's all it is. Just a room. A room with one square window high on the back wall which exposes nothing but a patch of blue sky. A bed. Two doors. One open, one shut.

He's standing before me again, tracking my eyes.

"The bathroom," he says when my gaze falls to the open door. He reaches above me, his face coming dangerously close to mine. So close his breath caresses my face. Or assaults it.

My wrists are released and my arms fall to my sides, causing me to cry out a little at the pain of it. Immediately my eyes snap to his. Will I be punished for that cry of pain?

He shakes his head at my unspoken question and I want to slump to the floor in relief.

"Kneel."

I drop to my knees without question, my eyes falling to the floor. It is concrete. Cold and hard. Out of my peripheral vision, his hand snakes toward me, cupping my chin and drawing my head upward. I keep my eyes down, not wanting to look at him, not wanting to see whatever is reflected in his eyes, and scared of the proximity of my face to his groin.

"Look at me."

I try, but I can't bring my eyes up. Tears roll down my cheeks. My eyes are stuck on a pebble encased in the concrete. It is red, and in stark contrast to the black, white and gray monotony of the rest. I hear the whistle of air and wince as a sharp sting inflicts the bottom of my feet.

I look up. I expect to see lust, sickened desire, but I don't. I can't decipher any emotion in his eyes at all. Maybe he has none. That scares me most of all.

My heart pounds as I wait for him to move. My eyes dance between his, unsure where to look, unsure if I can keep staring into the ocean of emptiness.

And then he leaves.

CHAPTER FOUR

MIA

Minutes pass before I rise to my feet. I feel like he is watching, studying me, so the first thing I look for is a camera. Sure enough, there's one protruding from the ceiling above the door. There has been no effort to hide it. It's there in plain sight, the blinking red light letting me know it is on. Is he staring at a screen watching me now?

I stretch. Not high into the air, but lowering myself at the hips, letting myself fold over my knees and relishing the strain of the muscles down my legs and lower back. It feels good to move. I twist and turn, forcing as much stiffness from my body that I can.

Moving to sit on the bed, I allow myself to bounce on the mattress as though I'm testing its softness. As though it matters. Springs groan. There is a single blanket folded at the foot of the bed. No pillow.

Walking into the bathroom, I take in the shower, toilet and hand basin. Another camera hovers in the corner. There are no shower curtains. No privacy. Liquid soap sits in a bottle off to one side. It looks out of place in the bluntness of the rest of the room, boasting hints of cherry blossom. Its color is offensive. So happy and bright.

Leaving the bathroom, I consider banging on the other door, the one that opens and closes only to let him in. I consider screaming and yelling at the glass in the little square window. But instead, all I do is lower myself to the ground, my back sliding against the wall as I return to the corner with the chains, hugging my knees to my chest.

The sky is so blue. I wonder if Mum and Dad can see the same patch of sky. I wonder if they're worried about me, if they know I'm missing or if they think I'm at work or visiting friends. Have I been gone long enough for alarm? Was I unconscious for minutes? Hours? Days? Is my story splashed across the local news?

The door opens and panic floods. I pointlessly search the room for somewhere to hide. There is nowhere but under the bed and he would find me in an instant.

"Don't say a word."

My eyes search out that one pebble in the concrete, the splash of red. I have an urge to cover my nakedness, cross my legs, cover my breasts with my hands, but I don't. Somehow, I feel as though he would get satisfaction from that action.

His feet are bare again as he pads across the floor. Worn threads of his jeans press beneath his feet and trail over the floor behind him. The scent of food wafts through the air, twisting my stomach. I didn't realize I was hungry, but the intensity of it almost doubles me over in pain. I lift my eyes hesitantly. He's carrying a tray which he places on the ground as he takes the only seat in the corner.

"Come. Kneel." He nods to an empty space in front of him.

A war battles inside me. I don't want to do as he says, I don't want to succumb so easily, but what other choice do I have? I know he is capable of hurting me. I know the sting of the lash. And, although it isn't that bad, I fear what else he might do.

He watches as this battle rages. I know he can see it on my features even though I do my best to hide it. His head tilts to the side curiously as though he's studying my reaction. Finally, I get to my feet and kneel before him. My stomach groans loudly.

"You hungry?" Even though he asks it as a question, I know he doesn't want an answer. He's already made it clear he hasn't stolen me for my words.

"First we need to clean up those wrists." He nods to where my hands are folded neatly in my lap. The submissive placement of them suddenly strikes me and I let them fall to my sides. His face twists into an expression I can't read as he holds one hand out, palm up. I just look at it. He shoves it a little closer, urging me to place my hand in his.

"I'm just going to clean off the blood."

His patience wears thin and he leans over to grab me,

jerking my wrist toward him, examining the red welts and the broken skin. "You're hurt."

No shit, I want to say. But the wounds are superficial. The skin is only broken because I twisted and turned in my restraints. I shake my head almost involuntarily as I correct myself internally. The skin is broken because he chained me.

He looks up, the lines in his forehead bunching together. "I don't want to hurt you, do you understand?" He peers into my eyes as if trying to ascertain my level of comprehension like one would a child. "And I won't hurt you as long as you do exactly what you are told." Gently, he wipes the dried blood from my skin, moving downwards to clean away the trails down my arms. "You are to be trained for pleasure. There will be no pain unless it is your choice to have it." He wipes across the broken skin as if to emphasize his point.

I flinch. But I don't pull away. I don't move.

Trained for pleasure. The words echo around my head. Pleasure. A sick feeling creeps inside. I've heard about human trafficking, stealing women to train them as sex slaves. But it doesn't happen to people like me.

After he finishes cleaning the dried blood, he bends down and picks up the tray, balancing it on his knees. I want to reach out and snatch the food like some sort of untamed beast. Instead, I simply stare at it. It's better than staring at him. Those eyes are unnerving.

There is an array of food. Cheese. A hard-boiled egg.

Salami. Crackers. Pickled onions. Even a little bowl of relish. It seems odd under the circumstances.

He picks up one of the crackers and dips it into the relish. "Open."

I look up at him and hope he can see the hatred in my eyes.

"Open."

When I don't, he asks, "Not hungry?"

I don't move. I just kneel there, hands folded in my naked lap, nipples prickling with the cold.

He puts the cracker down. "I know you're hungry. Your stomach has been rather vocal about it." He pushes the plate further out on his knee, tempting me. "There's no point in starving yourself."

I leave my eyes locked on his. Unwavering. Unblinking. I want to know why he has me. I want to know when I can leave, if I can leave.

"I can see the questions floating in your eyes. You're doing well not to voice them."

Well? I'm doing well? I want to laugh. I want to scream. I want to spit in his face.

He picks up the cracker again. "I'm not sure what point you are trying to prove by not eating." He sighs. "Maybe I should explain a few things to stop this stupidity. Maybe you have illusions that you might escape this, that it is temporary. Maybe you think that someone will come to your rescue."

He leans forward, his face in mine. The scent of him

34

invades me and I close my eyes for a moment before I start to tremble.

"You are here to be trained. You are here to learn obedience. You no longer belong to yourself. This is your future. This is your home. Obey me and your punishments will be minimal. Disobey, and you will learn the consequences. There is a camera trained on you at all times. You cannot escape. There is no point in trying. Now," he leans back again, lifting the cracker once more, "open."

And I do.

CHAPTER FIVE

MIA

I try to sleep. I lie down on the mattress and stare at the ceiling but my eyes refuse to shut. The blink of the red light taunts me. Is he watching? Is it just him or are there more?

The blanket offers little protection against the cold but at least it gives me some privacy to hide my nakedness. I wonder if he will take it from me when he realizes.

After a while, I give up on sleep and walk across to the spot in the corner where the chains dangle from the ceiling. Lowering myself to the ground, the coldness of the wall seeps through the blanket and into the skin of my back, but I can see the stars from here. I wish I had studied them. I wish I knew what each speck of light meant. I know there is a cross, a pot or a belt. But none of them form patterns in my head. To me, it merely looks as though someone has scattered them, thrown them like one might throw seeds on the dirt.

When I was little, I thought the night was God pulling a blanket across the sky. Tucking us in like children. The blanket had holes, tiny pinpricks that let the light of heaven shine through. I thought that was how he watched us at night. One of the stars would blink, temporarily lost to the darkness and that was when God peered through the crack. That was when He was watching.

But none of the stars blink.

I sing softly to myself, hoping the music will bring me comfort. But music and comfort have no place here. It sounds strange in the echo of the empty room. Too broken. Too woeful.

I think back to the times I shyly sung at my local bar, urged on by Roxy. There was a part of me that enjoyed the spotlight but also a part that wanted to hide in the shadows. It all seems so pointless now. Nothing more than a dream that has no place in this stark reality.

Silent tears slip down my cheeks. Thoughts of Mum and Dad come unbidden. They will be frantic by now. Not a day goes by when I don't see them, or at least talk to them. We're close like that. Being an only child living at home ensures it.

I think of them and wonder what they are doing. I wonder if they are asleep or if the worry of my disappearance is keeping them awake. I wonder if Mum's sitting in the bay window in her room, staring up at the same stars as I am.

I keep my thoughts locked on them until sleep takes me.

The brush of the door wakes me. The stars are gone and in

their place the sun mocks me with its happiness. My captor looks at me in the corner and then over at the bed, but he doesn't say anything about me still sitting on the cold floor.

"Don't say a word." He sits in the chair in the corner, one that is made of wood and metal and looks like it belongs beside a school desk.

"Come. Kneel."

I stand slowly, taking my time to obey his orders, my bones complaining. He doesn't chastise, just watches, nothing given away in his gaze. I lower myself before him, kneeling on the cold hard ground.

"Drop the blanket."

I close my eyes as though it will give me the strength to obey. His hand grips the blanket and tugs it away roughly.

"I don't like to ask twice."

He tosses it onto the bed and my eyes follow it longingly. It is my protection. Already I feel cold without it.

"When I come into the room and say those words, that command phrase, this is the position I expect you to take. I do not want to have to instruct you again. Do you understand?"

I nod.

"Good." He rubs his hands along his jeans, leaning back into the chair, almost as though he is going to relax, as though we are friends about to engage in conversation. When he folds his arms across his chest, it causes the sleeve of his shirt to rise and allows black ink to peek out. "One question."

I blink, confused by his words.

"One question," he repeats with a sigh. "You can ask one question."

I open my mouth and then close it again, unable to find my voice. He lifts his brows. The furrowed lines deepen. Judging from the creases on his face, he must be at least ten years older than me. Maybe more. But the creases around his eyes aren't as deep as the ones on his brow, as though his expression is more used to worry than happiness.

He clears his throat. "Well?"

"Why me?" The words just fall out. Not when, how, or who he is. Just, why me.

"You've been requested."

"Requested?" I repeat and he nods. "By who?"

Anger flashes in his eyes. "One question." His voice is low with an undercurrent of cruelty. Getting to his feet, he looms over me for a moment before walking to the other side of the room. "Crawl."

"Excuse me?" I splutter before I can help myself.

He pulls the lash from his back pocket and stalks toward me, flicking it to the ground so it falls from itself, growing in length. It is one of those retractable ones. One that can be hidden. One that can go unnoticed in the back pocket of his jeans. I scramble away, even though there is nowhere to go, but I'm filled with the need to escape. I cower in my corner, hugging my knees to my chest, hiding as much of myself as I can.

He strikes and pain sears across my shins. A tear rolls down my cheek. The pain is bearable but the humiliation is not.

"Look up," he commands.

My chin wobbles but I do as I'm told, lifting my eyes until they meet his cold ones. He lifts the lash again. I lift my chin. We stare, both daring the other to take it a step further, but his shoulders slump just a fraction and he walks back to the chair in the opposite corner. He sits down and places the lash on the floor beside him.

"Crawl." He crosses his arms and leans back, waiting.

I found a dog once. I was only ten at the time and I knew my mother would never let me keep him, so I tried to hide him from her. I was convinced that if I could just keep him in my room, she would never know. But it was not a dog that was used to being trapped in a room. It was not a dog used to being indoors at all. So it scratched at the door, it whined and barked and I was so scared my mother would come home and find him that I yelled at the dog. I screamed and demanded that he stayed in the little bed I had made under mine. But the more I yelled, the more frantic I became, the less obedient he was. He darted away from me every time I approached, and I chased him around the room until I was breathless and frustrated. Then I just slumped against my bed and stared at him. The dog stared back, until finally, he crept across the floor, dragging his body as though he was crawling, and sat at my feet in submission. It wasn't until I gave up that the dog let me win.

Now I am the dog. But the man before me would easily outrun me. He would out-maneuver me. Overpower me.

I study him again, trying to burn his features into my mind. His lips are full and soft, in direct contrast to the rest of his appearance. His eyes are sunken and hooded with darkness bruising the skin beneath. The shape of them turns down at the edges, marring him with melancholy even though at the moment they are spiked with curiosity.

He is watching. Waiting. Interested to see my response to his command. His eyes shift to the lash on the floor and then back to me with a question. "The choice is yours," he says finally.

Choice. As if I have one. I have a choice between options but true choice was taken from me the moment I woke in this hellhole.

I'm pretty sure I could sustain quite a few lashes before he would break me. In fact, I'm not sure if he could break me with the lash alone. And that scares me. If I don't obey now, if I don't bend to his will, what other methods will he choose?

He is the one with the choice. Not me.

Without removing my eyes from his, I rock forward onto my knees and drop my hands to the floor. I begin to crawl. He shifts in his seat, uncrossing his arms and resting his hands on his thighs, straightening his back.

I keep crawling until my head nearly rests on his knee and then I rock back, kneeling before him again, my gaze still locked on his.

His eyes narrow. He swallows. "Are you hungry?"

I don't say a word.

He nods once and gets to his feet. I don't shy away from his closeness. Instead, I raise my head and continue to stare at him.

"Wait here."

I would go somewhere else in a heartbeat. But I can't. I'm trapped here with whoever this man is, to be whatever I am requested to be.

I don't watch as he leaves. I look at the small red pebble caught among the shades of gray and wait for his return. He brings fruit this time. Pineapple, melon and grapes. He clearly doesn't want me to starve.

Unmoved from my position, he sits before me again, taking a knife from his pocket and slicing into a thick chunk of pineapple. The blade glistens, calling to me, but when I move my gaze back to him, he is watching, a slight look of amusement on his face at my obsession over the knife. He knows what I am thinking.

"Open."

I obey.

He feeds me, placing a juicy piece of pineapple into my mouth. Instantly, I salivate with the sweetness. Placing the knife on the ground, he reaches forward and rubs his thumb over my jawline before gripping my chin viciously and pulling my mouth open once the pineapple is gone. His thumb, rough and calloused, slides over my teeth, dipping into my mouth and pulling my jaw down further. The pad of his thumb is wet when it runs over my bottom lip roughly. He runs it back and forth, pushing the sag of my lip from side to side before cupping my cheek.

I stay frozen, nothing moving apart from my eyes which remain locked on him, only moving when he does. He flicks his gaze between my eyes and where his hand drags over my skin, molding and bending it to his will. Exploring lower, I'm reminded of the sensitivity of my situation when his fingers wrap around my throat. Even though my heart is pounding, even though terror is flowing as blood through my veins, I keep my eyes locked on his. I don't want to succumb. I don't want to show my fear even though he has already seen it.

The pressure on my neck increases and his eyebrow twitches as though challenging me to look away, challenging me to submit to his unspoken threat. I blink once. His hand moves back up until his fingers dig into the soft flesh under my jaw. He tilts my head from side to side as if examining me, and then his hand falls lower.

I want to close my eyes. I want to escape his cold expression as the roughness of his hands causes my skin to prickle. He leans forward when he palms my breast, his eyes only inches from mine. Then his gaze follows the fall of his hand as he flicks his thumb over my nipple. It hardens. I want to curse my body for its betrayal, especially when his eyes move back to mine and a smirk teases the corners of his mouth. He leans back in the chair, slouching so his legs move further apart and rests his hands behind his head. One eyebrow flicks upward in amusement.

"What's that look supposed to mean?"

For a moment I forget. For a moment I am concerned about his opinion of me, and it sickens me. I don't let my fear show, though I'm sure he notices the gulp of air I swallow nervously as I wait to see if I will be punished for speaking.

His gaze scans my body as though it's the first time he's noticed I am naked. He shakes his head. "Nothing."

My body is taut but inwardly I slump with relief.

Reaching down, he plucks a grape and holds it before me. "Open."

He feeds me each piece of fruit until the plate is bare. Apart from the knife. It is large and sharp. If he's brought it here to frighten me, it hasn't worked. All I can think about is using it on him.

Then he instructs me to stand and I obey without hesitation. There is some part of me that believes him when he says he doesn't want to hurt me. But there is also a part of me that is terrified of what he'll ask me to do. I push that part to the side. There is no point in listening to it. Not yet. But it scolds me for giving in so easily.

Getting to his feet he takes my wrists in his hands and

pulls them high over my head, replicating the position I was in when chained.

"Stay."

My head nods before I can stop it.

Both hands begin to slowly move down my body, tripping over my elbows, caressing my arms, trailing down my sides, over my hips, his head following suit as he lowers himself until he is on his knees before me.

I swallow the fear lodged in my throat and do my best to think about something else. Anything else. But the feel of his hands on my skin allows for no escape. It grounds me to reality, forcing me to watch.

His hands rest on my thighs, head level with my stomach.

My heart is beating out of my chest as his eyes rise inch by inch over the swells of my body until they meet my mine again. His breath is hot on my flesh. I'm sure he can feel me trembling under his touch.

His eyes do nothing to betray his intentions.

And then he presses his lips to the small rounding below my belly button. Just the faintest of touches. The whisper of butterfly wings.

Tears form and spill. He looks up and one splatters onto his cheek. Letting me go, he captures it with this thumb and sucks it dry. Then he gets to his feet, stepping back as though nothing has happened. As though we aren't trapped in a room, me naked and exposed as he forces me to suffer his touch.

"You may lower your arms."

I cross them over myself trying to hide what little I can, but he shakes his head and pulls them apart. "Don't cover yourself. Ever."

My hands fall to my sides.

"You may ask another question."

Without hesitation, I ask, "Who?"

"Who?" he repeats, those grooves in his forehead increasing.

"Who requested me?"

He shakes his head, walking over to the tray left abandoned on the floor, the one holding the knife. "I can't answer that." He picks the tray up, holding it flat down the side of his body. "You may ask another."

I swallow the knot of dread at the back of my throat. "Do I know him?"

He's at the door by this stage, waiting with it half open. I try to move so I can see outside, but he closes it, leaving me alone with his answer.

"Well, he certainly knows you."

CHAPTER SIX

MIA

Standing under the scalding hot water, I almost feel normal. Whatever that means. Normal is standing in the shower and letting the water fall over my body. Normal is getting out and drying myself with a towel. Normal is wrapping that towel around my damp hair and stepping into my bedroom to get dressed. Pulling on clothes. Heading to work.

Those things are normal.

What my life is now is not.

If I close my eyes and let the water stream over my face I can imagine I'm back home. The scent of chlorine that lingers after my morning swim. The swirl of steam as it gathers near the vent, too eager and too thick to pass through the small opening. The patch of mold that clings to the ceiling no matter how hard I scrub. The small mark on the mixer that indicates when the water is the perfect temperature. Right between freezing and scalding.

But scalding is my chosen temperature now. I want it to burn, cleanse my skin of all the filth. Purge it of his touch.

Once my skin is pink and my hair smells of cherry blossom, I sink to the bottom of the stall, letting the water rain down on me until it turns cold.

He knows me. It doesn't seem possible. No one springs to mind. I do not know the type of people who would do this sort of thing. But then again, I guess no one does. The evil of this world does not wear a sign. There is no mark of Cain. But surely, if I knew someone capable of this, I would have sensed it. Evil would have surrounded them like a cloak, dark and thick.

I'm shivering. The water has turned from cold to freezing and I've lost track of how long I've been sitting here. My body protests when I get to my feet. It is as though it's ready to just give up and stay here. Let myself die from hypothermia.

There is no towel, so I leave puddled footsteps when I walk back in the room, stopping in my tracks when I notice he is there, waiting for me on the chair, towel resting over his knees.

"Don't say a word." There is less conviction in his voice, as though he is already weary of saying it.

Discovering that he isn't responsible for my captivity makes me fear him a little less. Makes me a little bolder. Any punishment he's dished out so far is bearable, so I just stare at him, the puddle of water at my feet growing. He sits forward, reaching toward his back pocket and I drop to my knees.

He nods and tosses the towel over me. "Dry yourself before you get ill."

I wrap the towel around my shoulders and relax into my motionless pose.

"Dry yourself and discard the towel." His conviction is back.

I remain unmoving, eyes locked on his. He stands and stalks behind me. Pain cuts into the soles of my feet as he lays a single lash across them. But still, I don't move. He strikes again. And again. Tears form in my eyes but the coldness has numbed me a little.

And the pain isn't so bad.

Mum has always said I have a high tolerance for pain. When I was little, a childhood friend and I were outside, climbing a tree. I fell out and crashed onto the ground, my arm pinned beneath me. My friend told me not to tell so we wouldn't get it trouble. I wiggled my fingers, tested the movement and decided it was fine. It was three days before I admitted what had happened to my mother and she took me for x-rays. Not long after, I was modeling a purple cast, my wrist broken in two places. I never cried, never complained.

It's time to test her theory.

He hits harder, hard enough that a hiss escapes. But the pain is temporary, flashing then dissolving. And then the towel is whipped from my shoulders, the cold air hitting me harder than the lash.

"Stand!" he orders.

I don't move, I simply follow him with my eyes as he stalks around the room, but I refuse to turn my head, so I lose sight of him as he walks behind me. Strong arms wrap around my waist and jerk me to my feet. I go limp, forcing him to drag me over to the corner where he presses the button that lowers the chains to the floor.

My heart starts to pound in my chest, revisiting my decision to defy him. But then he changes his mind, stopping the chains as they dangle mid-air. With me still hanging limply in his arms, he walks over to the chair and heaves me over his lap. It's only then that I start to fight. But he is strong, a lot stronger than me. His legs pin mine in place as he bends me over his lap, curse words falling from his mouth as I struggle against him.

"Let me go!"

"The more you fight the more it's going to hurt."

I renew my efforts, straining against him, trying to kick my legs and thrash about. But it is pointless. I'm nothing more than a rag doll to him. And worse still, I can feel his hardness jutting into my hip. He's enjoying this.

Whack!

His hand strikes my wet backside and the pain is instant, worse than the lash, but still nothing I can't handle.

"Fuck you!" I spit.

Whack!

My entire body stiffens as the pain intensifies. I grit my teeth together as he strikes me again and again until finally, I let my body sag and I fall limply over his lap, submitting to his command. He pushes me and I fall to the ground. Wiping away the tears that betray me, I glare at him with all the intensity I can muster.

"Kneel." His voice is cold and dark.

I wince as my heels push into my backside, my eyes scanning the polished concrete for the familiar stain of red.

"I've already told you I don't want to hurt you, but I will, if that's what it takes. The choice is yours."

And there it is again. Choice. He keeps insisting I have one.

"I am happy to spank you again, if you wish. I rather enjoyed it." There is a hint of humor in his tone and I look back at him with all the hatred and defiance I can muster.

"Stand."

I get to my feet, anger seething beneath the surface of my movements.

"Don't move," he instructs, "or else we'll have to start this process all over again." He shifts himself to the edge of the chair, bringing himself close to me. The faint outline of his erection bulges against his jeans. I close my eyes.

"Open your eyes. Watch."

A sob burns at the back of my throat, but I force it down. Reaching behind me, his hands rest on the cheeks of my backside.

"Warm." He chuckles.

He tugs me forward but I resist, planting my feet firmly.

Looking up at me with those blue-green eyes, he shakes his head in warning. I step forward. He rests his forehead against my stomach, drawing in a deep breath that whistles through his nostrils, inhaling me.

"You are not your own. Your body no longer belongs to you. You will do as I command." He says it as a chant whispered against my skin. "Repeat," he orders as his lips press to my flesh, kissing me gently, kissing me as though he means no harm.

When I don't repeat his words, he tilts his head away and looks upward to meet my eye. "Repeat," he says again, this time more firmly. "You are not your own."

I swallow the knot of defiance. "I am not my own."

His head tilts back down and his mouth moves to the dip of my waist, above my hip. His teeth graze my flesh, biting softly before dissolving into a kiss. "Your body no longer belongs to you."

My voice wavers, the assault of his mouth on my skin far worse than the bite of the lash. "My body no longer belongs to me."

His grip on my backside increases as he tugs me forward and bends until his mouth is level with the apex of my thighs. His eyes travel up my body hungrily.

I'm trembling. From fear, from arousal...I'm no longer sure. There is something in the way he's looking at me that's set my skin on fire despite the fact that moments ago I was numb with cold. I want him to toss me over his lap and spank me, press the lash to the soles of my feet, anything but look at me the way is he.

His voice is gravel, vibrating through my head and sending confused waves of longing to every cell. "You will do as I command."

His breath dances over me and I feel myself getting wet. I beg it to stop. I want to squeeze my legs together, stop this feeling before it devastates me with shame. I swallow and close my eyes, whispering to the darkness, "I will do as you command."

I'm confused by the emotions crashing through me. It is as though someone else, something else, has invaded my body and commanded it to crave his touch.

And then his mouth is on me, gently at first, teasing and licking. His nails dig into my backside as he buries his face between my legs. His teasing and licking turns to sucking and biting, sending bolts of desire through me.

"No," I whimper as my body responds to his attention.

He groans, and it undoes me. It creeps up so quickly I am unable to stop it and I come quickly, pulsing against him, my hands unwillingly grabbing fistfuls of his hair as a wave of pleasure turns me to dust. I gasp. His movements slow, the sucking returning to licking, my body still throbbing. I push against his shoulders, pleading with him to stop.

He releases me and I stumble backward, scrambling across the ground until I reach the corner, pulling my knees to my chest and hugging them tightly.

He wipes his mouth with the back of his hand, eyes locked on mine, and gets to his feet. The outline of his erection is no longer faint. It strains heavily against his jeans but he does not come toward me.

"You may ask another question." There is no hint of desire in his voice. Nothing to speak of what he just did.

I remain with my arms wrapped around my knees, my eyes locked on the concrete floor. He waits a moment, maybe two, but I don't move. I don't lift my eyes to his. And I don't ask any questions.

CHAPTER SEVEN

MIA

Every time I think of it, nausea twists in my gut. But despite that sick feeling, I can't stop.

The way his eyes locked on mine before he lowered his head.

The feel of his tongue.

The way my fingers threaded through his hair.

The gasp that escaped.

The convulsing of my body.

How could it betray me like that? How could I possibly find anything about my situation pleasurable? But I did. And it shames me.

Even though the water is still cold, I step under the stream again, determined to wash him from my body. Wash away my betrayal. But it isn't as easy as rinsing it away because the memory is still there, trapped in my head.

I am inexperienced when it comes to physical relationships. I've only ever had one boyfriend who I was intimate with. He was the popular kid and I was the quiet girl at the back of the class who stared at him longingly, just like every other girl in the school. He had blond hair, blue eyes and the most endearing of smiles. It made me want to sigh and scream at the same time. But it wasn't until after high-school that we began to date. I'm not sure if he knew I even existed before that. But when he lost his scholarship due to smoking weed on the school grounds, Thomas Fuller became the cliché of the popular kid that was going places to the one who swept the floor at the local garage. He still played rugby but his chances of making it his career were over. And, as it turned out, he wasn't talented enough to make it on his own anyway. He was just popular.

But when he walked into the bakery one day, moody and feeling sorry for himself, I didn't see any of that. I just saw the boy whose face I had dreamed about for most of my high school years. My adoration inflated his downtrodden ego and we were soon dating. Five months we were together. Five months when I tried to convince myself that he was the man I had always wanted. Five months before I finally admitted he wasn't.

Could this be some sort of sick revenge? And if so, why was it a stranger who held me against him and brought me to a trembling mess with the stroke of his tongue?

My captor leaves me alone for the rest of the day, although I can feel him watching. The red light on the camera burns even when my eyes are closed.

I sleep in the bed that night but I move it so when I lie

down I can see the stars. They blink on and off so I know God is watching too. I wonder why he has abandoned me and then I remember that I have never turned to him in the past, so why would I expect him to save me now.

In my sleep I am safe. In my sleep there is nothing but darkness. I have no dreams, no faces that taunt me, but when I wake, he is there. Watching and waiting. Sitting in his chair which has been placed beside my bed. I sense him before I open my eyes. His scent. Sawdust and musk.

"Morning."

I open one eye to glance at him.

"You look peaceful when you sleep."

I risk speaking. He hasn't said the command yet. Maybe I am allowed to appear human. "It's because you're not in my dreams."

He lifts his eyebrows, deepening the creases in his forehead again. The lines fascinate me and I wonder what makes them so appealing. I wonder what made them so deep.

"You didn't seem to mind so much last time I came to visit."

Color creeps up my cheeks but I refuse to cower. I sit up and rest my feet on the cold ground, defiantly resisting the urge to cover myself.

"It doesn't change what you've done."

"And what exactly is it that I've done?"

"You've stolen me, chained me and forced me to do

things against my will. Just because my body betrayed me by doing what it did, doesn't give you the right to keep doing it."

"I am only acting on behalf of someone else."

I narrow my eyes, staring at him so hard I hope it hurts. "My requestor."

"Your requestor."

"Did he force you?"

"Force me?"

"Yes, force you. As in threatened you. Hurt you. Made it so you had no choice."

"There is always a choice. No one can take that away."

"I'll keep that in mind next time you're beating me into submission."

"Beating?"

"Yes. Beating," I spit back.

"I would hardly call anything I've done to you a beating. Many people do that sort of thing by choice."

"So you're admitting I don't have a choice?"

He rolls his eyes. "It could be worse, you know."

"Worse than stolen, chained and beaten?"

"A lot worse. You should be grateful."

"Grateful?"

"Yes. The man who requested you wants to love you. He wants to shower you with nice things and look after you. It's just that he has certain tastes and requires that you satisfy them. There are many men who would prefer you locked in a basement, use you for pleasure and for pain and little else. This man doesn't want that. You will have liberties if you please him. As long as you obey." He looks down at his hands locked between his knees. "It could be a lot worse."

"And it could be a lot better."

"But it isn't," he says, getting to his feet and breaking what little progress I thought we had made. And then he utters the command. "Don't say a word."

I get to my knees, hands in lap, eyes on the ground. I don't want to look at him. I can't look at him. When I do, there are too many mixed emotions. Shame. Fear. Disgust.

Longing.

After days of solitude, I've come to crave human contact and my heart flutters a little, leaving me confused. There is nothing particularly attractive about him, but certainly nothing unattractive either. I keep telling myself that it's only because of this forced isolation that I'm attracted to him. A type of Stockholm syndrome or something.

"Crawl." Even his voice does things to my insides.

I swallow the rebellion resting at the base of my throat and place my hands on the cold floor. I crawl in a circle around the room, eyes downcast. Humiliation combines with arousal.

"Stand under the chains."

I'm surprised at how quickly tears prick in my eyes. I don't want to be chained again. There is something more terrifying about it with the knowledge of experience. My wrists are still red from the chaffing from when I first arrived. But I place myself where he commands and try to stop my quivering from showing on the outside.

"Reach up and hold the chains."

I close my eyes and breathe in my relief before reaching up and grasping the cuffs that once surrounded my wrists. But it leaves me vulnerable and exposed, bringing back the memories of him standing so close. His mouth on me. The flush that ran over my skin.

My captor steps toward me, so close his scent invades me again. Only this time it's not sawdust he smells of. He smells of the outdoors. Of sunshine and rain. Of pine and grass. Of sea and sand. Of dirt and wind.

I breathe in deeply, not caring that he notices.

"Open your eyes."

Storm-filled eyes lock on mine. He reaches up and wraps his fingers around my wrists, his body parallel to mine, mimicking my stance, and then he begins to drag his fingers down my arms, exploring every inch as though looking for flaws.

"Look at me," he growls again.

I hadn't even noticed my eyes were closed. He's too close. It hurts to look into the coldness of his eyes as his fingers scrape over my skin. But I do as I'm commanded and force them open, mustering as much hatred into my glare as I can.

But it's hard to muster hatred when he sets my heart pounding like it does. His hands are on my sides now. They caress my skin, leaving goosebumps in their wake. Then they move to my back and he dips a little, his knees brushing against mine as he explores the flesh of my backside and thighs. He moves them in continuous motion, back up my spine and around my sides until they cup my breasts. And then it is his eyes that close, his breath that inhales when he digs his fingers into the soft flesh.

It almost hurts.

Almost.

But a hurt that feels good.

One that has me cursing myself for even thinking that way.

He travels downwards, over my stomach and when he lowers himself to his knees, my heart leaps in my chest. Fear and anticipation prickle over my skin. Inwardly I beg him not to touch me there. Not to feel the moisture and dampness.

He probes my thighs, sliding his hands between them before skimming higher. I let out an exhale of air I didn't know I was holding when he gets to his feet again, his face only inches from mine.

"You may bring down your arms. You are doing well."

I snort then immediately cut it off, fearful of his reaction.

"It's time to add a little something to your training." He takes a step back, allowing me to breathe. "When you receive a command, you are to reply with, 'It is my pleasure to obey your command.'"

I look at him, my eyes narrowing.

"Say it."

"Why?" I whisper.

Anger lights his eyes and tightens his stance. "Say it."

"It is my pleasure to obey your command," I mumble.

"Say it like you mean it."

"But I don't."

"Pretend."

I want to spit in his face. I want to claw out his eyes and bite his nose. Strength – or maybe it is stupidity – boils beneath the surface of my skin. The violence of my emotions is exhausting.

"Why do you want me to say it when we both know it is a lie?"

He's surprised by my challenge. I can tell by the way he cocks one eyebrow, but he still answers. "Because it is what he wants. And you will do as he commands."

Seeing the defiance in my eyes, he takes a deep breath and offers an explanation. "I assume you're a smart girl, but even so, I'm going to make this simple for you. Do as you're told and you won't get hurt. That's it. Obedience. That's all that is required of you." He walks further away from me, across the room and folds his arms, waiting patiently. "Say it."

I've always been a good girl. Mum never had to spank me, never even had to raise her voice. If I ever thought about disobedience she could tell, and she would look at me with such disappointment, I would cave.

But that need to obey has left me. I can't do it anymore. I can't meekly submit to his commands. He hasn't hurt me that much, yet. I can handle more. So I decide to test the boundaries and turn away from him, facing the wall. My body trembles as I await the backlash.

Boldness dances over my skin as he steps behind me. The heat of his body warms me as his lips brush against my ear.

"Turn around." It is a command and a growl.

I stay frozen. The heat of him dissipates.

"Turn around!" His voice bounces off the walls, causing me to flinch with its controlled fury.

But still, I don't move. Even though my heart is pounding, my hands are slick with sweat and my knees are weak, I keep facing the wall.

I don't hear him get out the lash, but I hear it whistle as it whips through the air and lands on my backside. I wince as the pain slices through me. But I can handle it. I just need to switch off. Think of something else. Again and again the lash whistles then lands on my flesh. Even without seeing it, I know there are raised and angry red welts. But they don't hurt. Not really. They sting, but the feeling is fleeting.

He breathes heavily, words falling from his mouth as he snaps. "Turn around!"

Gritting my teeth, I steel myself. I am becoming numb, his attempt to punish me almost laughable. Gathering courage, I lift my chin and straighten my shoulders.

But the lash doesn't strike again.

My head jerks back violently as he grabs a fistful of my hair. "Don't be stupid," he hisses. "You can make this stop. All you have to do is obey."

His elbow slams against my back and I am pushed against the wall, my breasts taking the brunt of the impact.

"I will put you back in those chains."

Fear twists like a knife in my gut but I hold strong, determined to test just how far he will go to ensure my obedience.

"Ah," he says, feeling my body tense. "You don't like that idea, do you? Did you feel hopeless in the chains? Exposed?" He twists me around roughly, demanding that I look at him.

I look at the window.

I look at the door.

I search for the patch of red on the floor.

He grabs my jaw, forcing the direction of my gaze.

I close my eyes.

And then his mouth is on mine. Rough. Demanding.

I force myself not to respond. I don't react. And I certainly don't move my lips against his.

He cups the sides of my face painfully as his mouth devours me, insisting on obedience. He sucks my lower lip into his mouth. I let my body fall slack against the wall and he digs his knee between my legs, forming a resistance to my intention of crumbling to the ground. His teeth graze my lip but garner nothing. Not a wince. Not an intake of breath. And then he bites before releasing, his forehead pressed against mine and his heavy breaths hitting my face.

"Please." His voice is torn and broken. Nothing like it was before. Nothing like I expected. "I don't want to hurt you."

My eyes move to his but they are blurred with closeness.

"Please," he begs again.

And then, after taking a deep breath, he lets me go and I allow my body to slide to the ground, pulling my knees to my chest and hiding my face in the crevice.

My backside is tender against the concrete but the coldness lessens the sting. A breath of air washes over me as the door opens and closes and I am left alone.

I suck my bottom lip and taste blood.

A spark of triumph blazes in my chest.

I won this round and in doing so realized something about my captor. He could have demanded my obedience with violence, but he didn't.

CHAPTER EIGHT

MIA

I don't move from my place huddled in the corner. The patch of blue sky visible through the small window is comforting. I allow my mind to wander back to my life, the one I knew before. There must be some clue, some hint as to who has requested me, and I am determined to figure it out. If nothing else, it gives me something to think about other than where I am, and why I'm here.

I think of the men in my life but I can't even consider any of them to be guilty. It's simply not possible. The men I know are good men, kind men. Sometimes stupid men, but stupidity doesn't equate with evil, often stupidity indicates a lack of it.

My life was one of routine. I rose each morning at 6am and biked to the pool. There's nothing quite like the feeling of slicing into uncut waters. It's where I feel I can breathe the easiest even though my chest is compressed underwater. There's something hypnotizing about it. It's the one time I truly feel alone without feeling lonely. A place where I can block out the world and concentrate on nothing but the gasp and exhale of my breath and the burn of my muscles. But as soon as I stop, when my head breaches the water and my feet find the ground, the serenity is lost. There are swimmers in other lanes. Lifeguards at their stations. Children splashing. Parents watching. And as much as I relish the sharp gasps for air and the elongated exhales that create bubbles underwater, I still need to stop every now and then. My lungs demand it.

And that is where I usually find him. The only person that springs to mind as someone who makes me uncomfortable, though the thought of him capable of something as evil as imprisoning a person, still doesn't sit right with me. It's hard enough for me to comprehend that it has happened, let alone the possibility of it being someone I know.

He is a regular at the pool, like me. We started off smiling and nodding, but over the few months we've been swimming at the same time, a sort of friendship developed.

Sort of, because I didn't know what to make of him at first. I still don't. He is around my age but seems older because of the way he speaks. So soft, so gentle. He has dark hair splattered across his chest and sitting as a heavy mop on his head. He wears a bathing suit that is too small and too tight. He seems friendly enough but there is something about the way he looks at me that makes me feel uncomfortable. I feel bad for even thinking that, as he has been nothing but sweet, often commenting on my stroke and the way I cut through the water like a swan. I pointed out to him once that swans don't swim, but he still insisted on calling me one.

Can you accuse someone of evil merely because of the way you feel around them? There is no evidence that he could be my requestor. I know nothing about the man. Not even his name. Yet there were times that he looked at me and my skin crawled.

And then there is the man at the coffee shop. Man or boy. I'm not sure. He has blond hair which hangs in his eyes and a hesitant smile. Each day when I stop for my afternoon coffee, he is there. The first time I saw him he offered to buy my drink. I politely declined. The next day when I arrived, he was already waiting, my long black with cream ready in his hands. He asked me on a date. I said no. But he is a persistent man-boy and every day since, he has bought my coffee, even when I've asked him to stop.

Is this his way of getting what he wants? Was his small stature and hesitant smile hiding an evil lurking underneath?

And are they really the only two men I can think of that could be my requestor? Maybe I don't know them at all. Maybe he knows me without me knowing him. Maybe he has stalked me for months, watching my movements from afar, waiting for that perfect time to pounce. Even so, if that were the case, why isn't he here now? Why is there someone else who enters my room and commands me with his voice?

A memory flashes into my mind. One that was dulled with the slight buzz of alcohol.

There are two places to go for a drink in the town I call home, but only one which people under the age of thirty show their faces. And it was that bar that Roxy and I headed to that night. She had travelled down from the city with her brother and boyfriend for a night out in our small town.

It was through her brother that I had met Roxy. They were twins. Roxy and Remy. Roxy was sure her parents were high when they named them. Her brother and I had somehow been setup on a blind date. It was a disaster. He was too quiet and sullen to be much company, but I did end up with a new best friend when his sister inadvertently crashed our date. Roxy and I had always meant to be together. She was everything sarcastic and rude but everything sweet and kind. We were lifelong childhood friends who just never met until they had grown up.

Since then, she has moved to my small town, renting a modest house and working at the local travel agents, much to her parents' disgust. They are city people through and through. They told Roxy they wanted more for her. But more to Roxy meant more rules, more boredom. She wanted to live her own life.

The bar was busier than usual that night, which meant there were maybe thirty people there. A live band that consisted of locals was playing on the small stage. I knew the members like I knew just about everyone else there. The man behind the bar had been the same person that served us when I was little and my parents brought me here for Friday night drinks. I used to play on the pool table while they and their friends laughed and drank the night away. I went to school with the barmaid. My father is friends with the men who sat at the slot machines. But there was a man who didn't belong. He was dressed all in black and leaned alone against the bar, bottle clutched in his hand.

Roxy insisted I sang that night. Just a single song as people laughed and drank and danced. The man kept looking over at me, his eyes stuck on me as though it pained him to look away.

He didn't say anything. He didn't approach, but there was something in the way he looked at me. Something hungry. I never saw him again, that I know of, but maybe he has been lurking in the shadows, waiting for his time to pounce.

I sit for so long with my arms wrapped around my knees and my back against the cold concrete wall that my shoulders ache. I stretch, testing my muscles, forcing them into submission. Hours have passed, and he hasn't returned. I pace the room, not sure if I should be pleased my defiance has meant he has left me alone, or scared of what he is planning. So, when the door opens, I brace myself, prepared for punishment. But it isn't my captor who enters.

Instead, it is another girl.

ryker

CHAPTER NINE

RYKER

I knock and wait. There is only silence on the other side of the dark mahogany doors. I've been summoned but I know better than to enter without invitation. Glancing at my watch, I know I'm late. I wasn't when I arrived but now the clock has ticked past his specified time. Maybe he's decided he no longer needs me.

Then his voice reaches through the cracks. "Enter."

Pushing open the doors, I stride through the doorway and over to stand before his desk, hands behind my back, feet spaced apart like a soldier at ease.

"Ah, Ryker. You're here."

Mr Atterton sits behind his desk, leaning back in his leather chair, hands resting behind his head and one ankle hooked over his knee. No matter what the situation, he always looks relaxed. I think he does it to unnerve people. The more nervous they get, the more relaxed he becomes. Then, just as they are beginning to feel comfortable, he will surprise them with uncoiled aggression.

But not me. I've worked for the family for too long. I know how things work. I'm not fooled by his laid-back appearance.

"Yes, sir." I nod and stare at the oversized painting that covers the wall behind him. It's Grace. The horse that started it all. The one with which his father made his first million. It's easier to look at her than at him. The under-wrinkled and over-tanned skin stretched over his face reminds me of a corpse.

Mr Atterton gets to his feet slowly and strolls around to the front of the desk, leaning against it and crossing his arms. "Take a seat." He nods toward the plush leather chair behind me. I sit, but I don't relax my stance like he does. I'm on duty. Unlike the image Mr Atterton portrays, I'm always alert.

It's only as I lower myself that I notice the girl kneeling at the side of his desk. She's naked. There's a collar around her neck, the chain attached padlocked to the leg of his desk. Her eyes are trained to the ground. The left side of her face is swollen, the imprint of Mr Atterton's hand outlined in red. Thick bloody lines run down her forearms as though someone has dragged their nails across her skin. She is beautiful. But they always are. His collection.

He sees the direction of my gaze and chuckles. "Don't mind her. She's here to learn a lesson. Can't be trusted to be left to her own devices." He pushes himself off the desk and walks over to her, reaching for her arm. She doesn't shy away when he lifts it high above her head, holding it out for me to inspect. "She forgot that her body is no longer her own." He lets her arm flop back to her side then pats the top of her head. "Over the next few days she will remain here, under my watchful eye until she can be trusted not to hurt herself again. Isn't that right, my love?"

She moves for the first time, but only her eyes. They flick upward, acknowledging his words. "Yes, Master."

He presses a kiss to her head, lingering as though he's inhaling the scent of her and whispers in her ear. I don't hear the words, but from the way her body stiffens I know they are not words she wants to hear.

Walking back to resume his position leaning on the desk, Mr Atterton squares himself before me. "I've got somewhat of an unusual request to make of you."

He likes to use the word request. It implies choice.

"Whatever you need." It's my standard response.

He lifts himself away from the desk and walks over to the window. Below him, a horse races around the track, the trainer timing each lap and stable boys eagerly watching with their arms hooked over the railing. He falls silent and I wonder if there is something I am supposed to say. But Mr Atterton is comfortable with silence. He often pauses mid-sentence, waiting for the other person to grow nervous before continuing.

Then, as if shaking himself from a reverie, he turns back to me. "Junior has made somewhat of an odd request." And there's that word again. Request. The Attertons' don't request anything. They demand.

"Something I can help you with, sir?"

Mr Atterton considers himself a collector and I'm often asked to source the things he wants. Even though officially, I'm his personal bodyguard, I occasionally travel, finding the beautiful objects he craves then hides away in the dark hallways and rooms of this house. People claim his collection rivals many museums. But it's not a museum. It's a mausoleum. A place to take the pretty things of this world and bury them.

Reaching back over his desk, he slides a photo from a plain manila folder and holds it out. It shows a girl, young, late teens-early twenties at a push. She has dark hair, dark eyes, full lips. She is beautiful. My insides twist a little at the thought of what he is going to ask me to do, but I push the feeling away. I'm good at doing that. Switching off. It comes in handy in this line of work.

"Her name is Mia Cooper."

I scan the documents, raising my brows in surprise when I see she's a local girl, living only a couple of hours away. Not something he would usually mess with. The Atterton family business has many fingers in many pies, but they mainly deal in two trades. Horses and women. To the outside, they are known for their horses. But to a few, to the criminal underworld they dabble in, they are known for the auctions they host late at night. People from all over the world descend to peruse the goods on offer, trading, selling and swapping. The Attertons' themselves are more of a boutique compared to the large operations of the people they deal with, but the isolated location and alternative reason for business make the mansion the perfect gathering place.

I hand the photo back without comment.

"I know it's beyond the scope of what we normally do, but I want to indulge him. He's my son, my blood, and I'm feeling generous." He folds his arms across his chest. "But she cannot go to him untrained. She'd most likely not survive it. He has no patience, that boy."

I allow myself to chuckle. It's expected of me. Mr Atterton has made no secret of his only son's shortcomings. I'm expected to make fun of the kid, but only to a certain point. Junior is blood. He is an Atterton. I am not. But no patience is an understatement. Junior Atterton is used to getting what he wants. He's entitled and cruel, a dangerous combination. Not only that, but there is something different about him. Something off. I've never been able to pinpoint exactly what it is about the boy, but there's this uncharacteristic calmness to him, despite his proclivity for anger. He's also an undeniably talented pianist, something which has my sister enthralled.

"I will need you to do it."

I blink and clear my throat. "I'm not sure I quite understand, sir."

"I need you to train the girl," he states plainly, leaving no room for misunderstanding.

"But won't Junior want to train her himself?"

"I've talked to him, he understands. He knows this is the only way I'll agree to it."

I push a little further. "Surely you have men more skilled to take on the job. Marcel maybe, or Winston."

Mr Atterton trains a few girls a year, just a small selection of girls that usually come from far away. His trainers would know what to do. I do not.

He shakes his head and walks back around the desk to take his seat. Dropping his hand, he clicks his fingers. The girl crawls to him and he rests his hand on her head.

"He doesn't want those brutes near her, and if I'm honest, I don't blame him. The trainers are used to a certain amount of freedom and perks in their position. They like to taste the goods. Ensure their quality." He winks. "That cannot happen with this girl. You are the only one I can trust not to maim, fuck or hurt her."

I shift uncomfortably in my seat. I have no idea about training. Not with horses or with girls. There are too many things that could go wrong. Too many mistakes that I could end up taking the blame for. "My only fear is that my inexperience would somehow hinder her."

His eyes whip in my direction and I brace myself for the lash of aggression, but it never comes. Instead, he turns to the one subject he knows will ensure my obedience.

"Your sister called this morning. She seems to be going

well, enjoying herself. Have you heard from her lately?"

"I spoke to her over the weekend."

"And she seems to be happy, yes?" His eyes fix on mine, saying all the things his words don't. And that's all it takes. Just the mere mention of her, the unspoken threat, and I know I can't refuse.

Choosing to look at the girl rather than me, he strokes her hair as he continues to speak. "This means a lot to my son and therefore it means a lot to me. For whatever reason, he wants this girl and I am determined to give her to him. My son might be an entitled prick who is quick to anger, but he is my son. What he wants, he gets. You could almost call it our family motto." He chuckles at his own joke. "It has to be you, Ryker. You are the only man I trust with this." He reaches into the manila folder again. "Here is a list of instructions and commands that Junior wishes for the girl to know by the time she gets to him. Cameron has already collected her, and she is at Silver Oaks waiting for you."

Reaching over to take the piece of paper, I scan over it. Junior has scrawled a simple list complete with commands and demands. Her skin is never to be broken. I am never to draw blood. He wants her trained in silence. She must assume a certain position on the command, 'Don't say a word.' She must respond to commands with, 'It's my pleasure to obey you,' and she must mean it.

They were specific and strange. Just like the boy.

"By the time she gets to him, she must obey basic

commands. She can't shy away from being touched or hesitate in any manner. I need her to last longer than a few months. You can do whatever it takes to ensure this, as long as you follow Junior's rules. You might have to get creative. And, of course, it goes without saying, but I will say it anyway so there can be no misunderstanding between us." He dips his hand into the girl's mouth, yanking her chin down violently. He looks at me directly as the girl kneels beside him, her mouth gaping open. "Your cock is not to enter any part of the girl. Do you understand?"

I clench my teeth together, insulted that he would even suggest such a thing. Forcing a girl held captive may be his style, but it certainly isn't mine.

"Yes, sir."

"You can indulge yourself with hand jobs, that's fine. But nothing else." He withdraws his thumb from where it was hooked over the girl's teeth and tells her to stand. "Get her used to being touched." He runs a hand down the girl's arm then grabs one of her breasts roughly. "Touch her often. Bring her to orgasm. Get her used to being used, but do not abuse her. She is not yours."

He's standing in front of the girl now and bends down to take her breast in his mouth. I shift uncomfortably, but it's nothing I haven't seen before. Mr Atterton doesn't hide from me. There is no need to. Unlike others, I know every aspect of his life. Nothing is hidden because I am loyal. He's ensured it.

When he finally moves away from her, there is a single tear rolling down her cheek and a ring of red around her nipple. Atterton thumbs her cheek, wiping the tear and feeding it back to her.

"I'm counting on you, Ryker. Do not let me down."

"Yes, sir." I nod once in acknowledgment and get to my feet, eager to leave before his attention to the girl becomes more amorous.

CHAPTER TEN

RYKER

Silver Oaks is one of the smaller stables dotted around the country that the Attertons own. The stables hold around a dozen horses. There is no grand house, no surrounding farm, just the stables and a track in the middle of nowhere. But under the stables are four cells and in one of them the girl waits.

I grunt in acknowledgment at the greeting of some of the trainers and make my way to the rear of the stables, disappearing down a hidden set of stairs to bang loudly on a door. Marcel opens it within seconds.

"I'll need the code," I say before he can speak.

"It's great to see you again too." Marcel's words are mumbled around a toothbrush, his sarcasm thicker than the foam at the corners of his mouth.

We've met a few times before. None of them were pleasant. Marcel likes to talk. I don't. Marcel likes company. I don't. Marcel likes to detail how he trains his girls. I don't like to listen. My position within the family allows me power over him. Marcel doesn't like that.

Despite the fact that he opened the door, he stands in my way, shirtless, toothbrush running back and forth over his teeth.

"Are you going to move, or should I make you?"

Marcel rolls his eyes and turns. "Always so aggressive. What happened? Mummy didn't love you enough?"

His accusation hits close to the truth and I step toward him, not being able to help the smirk that crosses my face when he shies away, his hand dropping from the toothbrush, leaving it hanging limply from his mouth.

"Let's get things straight here and now," I growl. "I'm here to do a job that Mr Atterton requested of me. Nothing more, nothing less. There is no need for any interaction between us other than what is necessary. You do your thing and I'll do mine. Okay?"

Marcel grins and the toothbrush bounces. "Sounds like someone missed me." His mouth puckers and he blows a kiss. A speck of foam hits my face. His grin drops as I wipe it from my cheek.

"Where is she?" I ask, striding down the hall. I dump my bag on the floor, the one that contains my entire life, well, the parts I own, anyway, and stare at the monitors. Each of them are trained on a girl in a cell.

Marcel taps the first screen with the base of his toothbrush. "That one."

She sits on the ground, propped against the wall, chains

around her wrist.

"What did you do to her? She looks fucking dead."

Marcel grins, finally swallowing then licking his lips clean. "She should wake up soon. Cameron gave her something to help her sleep. Isn't he nice?"

I frown and pull out a seat to sit in front of the monitors, propping my feet on the desk. "You can go."

Marcel shuffles from the room, stopping before walking into what I assume is the door that leads to our accommodation. "Remember, I'm the one with experience here. You may need help. Don't be too quick to dismiss me."

I keep my eyes stuck on the screen until he leaves. I won't be asking the bastard for anything. I never ask for help. Ever. Not even when I need it.

The girl on the monitor is beginning to wake. She pushes her legs along the ground as though she's stretching her muscles. Then she starts to thrash violently, testing her restraints, twisting and pulling against them until she breaks skin and trickles of blood run down her arms.

"Fuck." The first of Junior's rules have already been broken. What was Marcel thinking when he put her in chains? She isn't like the others. She can't be treated the same. But the damage is done now. Her skin is already broken. I decide to leave her for the time being and just watch without interference. Reaching into my bag, I tug out the manila folder. The girl's name is Mia. I hate that name.

One of Junior's aunties is named Mia and she's the vilest bitch I've ever come across. She took a particular shine to me, assuming she could make demands of me like the rest of the family did. But Senior Atterton set her straight and for that I was grateful. Even though I despise the rest of the family, I can't help but have a level of respect for the guy. Respect and gratitude. Begrudging respect and gratitude at times, but it is there.

Leaning forward, I adjust the volume, lifting it until the sounds of her screams fill the room. The reality of what has been asked of me begins to sink in. I wish there was a way I could've refused, but saying no wasn't an option. I don't just owe them my life. They own it. Every fucking aspect of it.

Resigning myself to my fate, I get to my feet, making my way over to her cell. The door is heavy, made of a soundproof material that breaks the tightness of the air when opened. She stops screaming when I enter. Her head whips around, trying to find the source of the noise. She calls out hello. She's still sitting on the ground, darkness shielding her eyes, hair in disarray, lips plump and full.

Fuck. She's even more beautiful in the flesh.

Junior's tastes usually steer toward blonde with big tits. But this girl is different. She's the sort of wholesome beauty you only find in small towns. The sort that has no fucking clue how gorgeous they are.

Despite staying still, she knows I'm here. She keeps calling out, talking to me as though I will help. Her naivety is amusing. She hasn't tasted darkness and cruelty in her life like I have. I almost feel sorry for her. But pity is a useless emotion in my profession. Pity. Empathy. Sadness. Nothing good ever comes from them. The sooner she learns her fate the better, because hope is another pointless emotion.

There's a button in one corner of the cell that lifts the chains until she's stretched on her toes. Thinking there's no better time to start her training, I run my hands over her, remembering Senior's words to get her used to being touched. She stiffens but doesn't object too much until my fingers reach the waistband of her jeans and then she screams. It's a piercing scream that causes me to reel away from her.

She doesn't stop. It fills the room, echoing off the walls until I shove her, pushing my elbow to her throat to cut off the noise. She kicks, feet, knees and legs flailing through the air until she connects with my shin. Bitch.

Regaining my composure, I grab her by the throat, pushing her back against the wall as I tear the clothing from her body. Buttons fall to the ground. My knife slices through the material of her bra.

For a moment, I am distracted by the perfection of her and let her go. She swings from the chains, her arms stretched above her, her breasts on display, perk and ripe and begging to be kissed. I curse inwardly. This isn't supposed to happen.

I've been at Atterton's side as he attended the auctions.

I've seen the girls. Naked. Dressed in leather. Dressed in lace. Dressed in silk. Bound and gagged. Chained. On leads like pets. But I'd never felt the slightest attraction to any of them. They looked more like dazed sheep than humans. Dull and lifeless eyes. Limp. Why anyone would want that was beyond me.

So, my attraction to her comes as something of a surprise. Personally, I'd prefer someone just as fucked up as I am. Not someone to sit meekly at my feet and follow commands. Pushing thoughts of how her skin would feel under my tongue from my mind, I start to unbutton her jeans, ignoring her screams. I wrestle them down her legs as she twists and kicks. Her knee connects with my chin and I stumble backward, yanking the last of her clothing with me.

Now she's completely naked and my eyes roam her body hungrily. My eyes don't know she's not mine. All they see is naked flesh and pouting lips. She's trembling. Goosebumps cover her skin. I want to soothe them with my tongue.

Fuck. I'm screwed.

But Atterton's words sound in my mind. *Don't let me down.* They sound innocent enough if you don't know the man. But I do. And I know the punishment for my disobedience will be in the form of a pretty smile and innocence.

As I lower the chains, the girl huddles against the wall as though it will shield her from me. Her head jerks in different directions as she listens, both hoping and scared to pinpoint my position. Her chest heaves with heavy breathing but she doesn't scream anymore.

I leave her there and walk out into the hallway, choosing to watch via the monitor and let her sweat her fate for a little longer.

Marcel is sitting on a chair, stuffing a sandwich into his mouth. "She's a feisty one, huh?" he mumbles between bits of bread. "You should have slapped her around a bit. It helps them realize the gravity of their situation. Makes them a little easier to work with."

I don't answer and jerk the seat out from under him. "Go find another chair."

Marcel drags another chair over the concrete floor and it scrapes noisily. He dumps himself beside me as though we are friends watching a rugby game. He nods to the second screen.

"That one's Star."

The girl is skinny and blonde. There is bruising on her side, stained purple. "She's been here a while. Didn't sell at the last auction. I think she had too much spirit. They could see the defiance in her eyes." He grins, once again showing the bread between his teeth. "Pretty sure she'll fetch a good price next time though."

Wordlessly, my eyes move to the next screen.

"She's new," Marcel says. "Only been here a few days. Lots of work left to do. She's been fun so far."

The girl sits huddled in the corner, crying. Every so often she bangs her head against the wall repeatedly before letting it drop to her knees again. "Shipped all the way from Aussie, that one. I call her Danielle. Not sure why, but it suits her, don't you think?"

I just glare at him. But then I relent and nod to the next screen.

"Ah, Petal. I make up names for them all. She's hardly been any fun, too broken when she got here."

Getting to my feet, I swing my bag over my shoulder and nod down the hall. "Room that way?"

"I've got the bed on the right. You can take the left."

"There's only one room?" I'm not used to sharing a room. I'm not used to sharing anything.

Marcel blows me a kiss. "Welcome roomie."

The room is simple and sparsely furnished. There's a bed along each side, a small square of window that is ground level from outside, a bathroom off to one corner. It's basically the same as the cell, minus the soundproofing and chains. There are a few more comforts though. Carpet on the floor. A dresser for clothes. A TV screen in the corner instead of a camera. It's old and there's no remote so I reach up to press the buttons and flick through the channels. Cartoons. Marcel watches cartoons. Finally, I reach the channel which shows her.

She's fallen asleep, her body slumped, but I can see the rise and fall of her chest so I know she's okay. Well, as okay as she can be under the circumstances.

Pulling my bag open, I dump the few items of clothing I

brought with me into the dresser. They only fill one drawer. Lowering myself to the bed, I push off my shoes, content to study the girl as she sleeps.

She keeps jerking herself awake, panic flooding her movements as the realization of where she is dawns on her again. I suppose I should go back in there. I need to start her training. The command Junior wants me to use is, 'Don't say a word.' Upon hearing that, she's supposed to fall to her knees, hands clasped meekly in her lap and await the next command. Should be simple enough. All I need to do is let her know what's at stake, scare the shit out of her without damaging her. Knowing Junior's command means he wants her silent, I grab a handkerchief, recalling her screams last time I entered the room.

She doesn't heed the command. Of course. She tries to beg and plead with me as though I have the option of letting her go. Shoving the handkerchief into her mouth, I muffle her scream before it starts. Raising the chains, I lift her until she is stretched fully, her toes searching for the ground as she dangles.

She's fucking perfect. Her breasts heave with each breath she takes. They're calling out to me, begging for me to touch them. They would be more than a handful, just big enough that her flesh would bulge between my fingers.

For a moment I allow myself to imagine meeting her in a different place, at a different time, for a different reason. The appeal of her being trussed doesn't diminish, but in my mind, it is because she wants it, asks for it, enjoys it. Her body would arc toward me, desperate for my touch. She'd still be trembling, but it wouldn't be from fear.

Her skin is smooth under my finger. I follow the lines of her body, the curve of her hip, the swell of her waist until I am back where I began. But her body does not arc toward mine and she's scared of my touch. She's trembling, but it's from fear, not desire. The gag has panicked her and she begins to hyperventilate. I try to calm her, but what can I say? Anyone would be terrified in her position.

And she should be.

CHAPTER ELEVEN

RYKER

Because I left her dangling, the cuts around her wrists have grown worse. Fresh blood drips down her arms and I curse myself for my stupidity. Atterton texted a few minutes ago. Junior intends on coming at the end of the day to inspect his gift.

And her skin is broken.

"Why the fuck did you put her in chains?" I say, eager to ensure Marcel takes the blame.

"Because that's what I do. It's all part of my method. First, you've got to—"

I tune out. Already I've grown tired of him and I've only been here a few hours. He talks too much. He eats too much. And he doesn't seem to visit his girls often, choosing instead to spend time in front of the monitor, one hand stuffed down his pants. I told him if I find him like that again, I was going to chop it off. His hand. Not his dick. I have a feeling that a lack of dick would affect his work standards and Senior wouldn't stand for that.

His voice drones on and on and I'm almost tempted to turn up the volume on the girl sobbing in the corner. Anything would be better than the sound of his voice.

"Not what you expected, is it?"

It takes me a while to realize he's asked a question. I glance over at him, trying my best to look uninterested, but he doesn't seem to take the hint.

"The first one is always the hardest. They stick with you, you know?" He leans back, tipping the chair to balance only on the rear legs. "I still remember my first. She still appears in my dreams. Her tears. Her cries. So fucking human." A slight smile creeps over his face at the memory. "But you've got to stop thinking of them like that. You've got to break them. Destroy their spirit, just like they do with the horses." He balances on the two back legs of the chair, swaying precariously and I resist the urge to kick them out from under him. "What can I say? It's what the clients want. Preferably, I like a bit of fight, but apparently our clientele doesn't."

Turning my attention back to the monitors, I see my girl has twisted her legs over on themselves, making it even more difficult for her to maintain balance. "She needs the bathroom," I say, getting to my feet and talking over Marcel.

His arm bars my exit, his gaze traveling up my body to meet my eye, a hesitant smile in place as his arm disappears.

"Leave her," he says. "Humiliation is good. It's effective

and it doesn't leave them physically scarred."

A trickle of liquid runs down her legs.

Marcel laughs then turns back to me. "Have you got many tools?"

"Tools?" I repeat.

"Tools." He gets to his feet, disappearing into his room before returning with a hard suitcase. He flicks the locks and opens it. "Whips, lashes, handcuffs." He lists all the options on display, his fingers running over them reverently, the same way mine had run over her flesh. "Here," he pulls one out, "this might come in handy." He flicks the small stick toward the ground and it lengthens, extending out from itself. "This one stings like fuck, good for the newbies, but it's almost impossible to inflict any damage other than a welt which will vanish within a couple of hours. You won't even be able to break skin with it." He lashes it over his hand. Immediately a line of red appears but he's right, there's no serious damage. "Take it." He holds it out to me. "This is a good starting point. You need something to help break that girl. I don't think asking nicely is going to do it for you. And if it doesn't work, you move onto something harder, something more painful, more convincing."

I take the lash begrudgingly, knowing he is right.

"Try the soles of the feet. Hurts like the buggery." He grins and his tongue darts out to lick his bottom lip.

"I need to clean the blood and piss off her first," I say, briefly running a fingernail down the sole of my foot to check its tenderness before tugging on my shoes.

Marcel nods to a small closet. "Buckets, cloths, bedding, sheets, pillows and all that sort of crap in there. Yell out if you need a hand cleaning her up. I wouldn't mind getting close to her. I bet she feels like satin."

"Touch her and fucking die."

Marcel holds his hands up. "Whoa. Calm down, psycho. I was just messing with you. She's yours alright. I'm not going to interfere. Unless you want me to. You know," he lifts his brows up and down and winks, "double team her and all." He chuckles and walks into one of the girls' rooms before I can knock his teeth out.

I need to get her out of the chains and cleaned up before Junior arrives.

She's quick to obey this time. I guess that's what a few hours dangling in chains does. She's eager to get the gag removed from her mouth, but she flinches when I touch her. It's to be expected, it's early days, but she needs to learn to control it, be open to my touch. His touch.

I warn her, keeping my voice low and steady and she stills as I wipe her clean.

Not that I'll admit it to Marcel, but I'm grateful for the lash when she refuses to open her legs. It's quick and effective. Then I remove her blindfold and sit in the chair, waiting for her to regain her sight as she adjusts to the stream of sun blinding her through the window.

She twists in her restraints, the movement sliding the

muscles of her stomach under her skin. She's not overly muscly, it's only because her hands are still stretched over her head, elongating her. Her waist is curved and her belly has the slightest rounding, so sensual, just a hint of the lines of her muscles showing at the sides. Her thighs are shapely, and her calves are so tight I want to sink my teeth into them. Her dark hair is a tangled mess, but it's her lips that make me want to groan. So full. So sensual. Plump. Kissable. Fuckable.

I shake my head, clearing the dangerous thoughts that linger there. What am I doing? She's Junior's, not mine. And she's young.

According to her file, she's only a few years older than my sister, years younger than me. So I block the thoughts from my mind like I've trained myself to do.

But I do wonder what she thinks when she finally focuses on me. She doesn't know that I'm not the one who took her. Not the one who wants her.

The first thing she does is speak. Not a quick learner. I have to use the lash again, needing her to submit to me quickly, rather than draw the punishment out.

Unlocking her wrists from the chains, I command her to kneel. She falls to the ground without hesitation and inwardly I smile. Maybe she's not the slow learner I previously thought. Drawing her chin upward, I command her to look at me. Her eyes are swimming in moisture. Tears balance precariously until they trip over and spill down her cheeks. She drops her gaze to the ground and I whip the lash over the soles of her feet.

She's so tempting, kneeling before me. Her eyes are the darkest of browns. So dark they could easily be mistaken for black if not for the outline of her pupils. Defiance and curiosity dances in them. Questions hover behind her tears. I need to leave. I need to get away before the temptation of her is too much and I do something I regret.

Junior is already standing at the monitors, Marcel at his side when I walk back into the room. His eyes are glued to the screen, twinkling with depraved anticipation.

"You can't go in there," I say before he even notices me.

"I can if I want. She's mine," says the petulant child.

"Not yet, she isn't." I do my best to keep my voice calm and even like his father does. "You agreed to let me train her. Part of that includes not going in there. Not yet. Not this soon."

Anger flashes across his expression and he reaches for the gun holstered at his side, pressing it to the side of my head. It doesn't scare me though. Junior is impulsive and quick to anger, but he's not stupid enough to shoot his father's favorite employee.

"Get that out of my face," I growl.

"Make me," he hisses back.

And so I do. Moving quickly, I snake out my hand, grabbing his wrist and twisting it away from me, gaining control of both him and the pistol.

"Men who carry guns are cowards," I say to the back of his head as his body jerks lower with each increased twist of his hand. "If you're going to kill someone, be a man. Look them straight in the eye and plunge a knife into their flesh or lock your fingers around their throat. Any man can pull a trigger, but only a weakling chooses to."

I know his father will hear about this. I know that as soon as he's out the door, he will be on the phone, his whinging voice telling tales. But like me, Junior is not scared. He knows I'm not stupid enough to hurt him.

It would be the end of me if I did.

I loosen my grip and he twists from my hold, running his hands through his hair to smooth it and reaching for his gun.

"Tut, tut," I say, holding it just out of his reach. "You can have it when you leave."

Taking the bullets out of the chamber, I shove the gun into the waistband of my jeans. Marcel is doing his best not to laugh as Junior fumes, threatening to call his father.

"Go ahead," I say. "You know he'll agree with me."

Then a sinister smile crosses his angular face. "Everly called me last night."

My blood turns cold. Just the sound of her name on his lips is enough to send icicles of fear into my heart. It's one thing for his father to use her against me, but it's another thing when he does.

"She said to say hello." Crossing his arms, Junior turns

back to watching the girl in the cell. She's stretching, testing her muscles after spending so long trussed up. The monitor is in grayscale, so the injuries around her wrists aren't too obvious. I desperately hope Junior doesn't notice.

"She's beautiful, isn't she?" he says as she moves to the bed.

He says the words almost lovingly but the glint in his eyes is anything but. There's a wickedness there, and for a moment, I feel sorry for this girl who is to be handed over to him as a pet. His annoyance at our altercation is gone now and he's transfixed by the way the girl's breasts jiggle with movement. He strokes the screen as though it allows him to touch her.

"I've been watching her for months, just waiting. She has no idea." He rubs his hands together gleefully. "Have you heard her sing?" There is something in the way he looks at me, a challenge in his expression.

I shake my head, knowing it's the answer he wants. When does he think she would have had the chance to sing? Fucking idiot.

He looks back at the monitor, the aggression in his stance sated. "Her voice speaks to my soul." He looks at her with what some might mistake as love. "It won't be long until you're mine, my sweet songbird."

As soon as he leaves, Marcel turns to me, eyes wide. "She's to be given to the fucking boss's son?" He whistles low and long. "Oh, how I'd love to get my hands on her just to mess with him. He's so fucking stuck up the way he looks down on everyone, thinking he's better than us all when he's a fucking simpleton."

"Watch your language," I hiss at him because there's nothing else to say.

I'm a bastard like that.

CHAPTER TWELVE

RYKER

Marcel stands in the doorway to our bedroom, white bubbles foaming at the corners of his mouth as he brushes his teeth. He's talking. I can tell from the way he pauses, the way his mouth moves occasionally, and the way he cocks one eyebrow, waiting for my response.

I flick my eyes over to him and point to the headphones covering my ears. They are noise canceling ones. And they are my new favorite thing.

I haven't been back in to see the girl since Junior left. His visit shook me a little, made me remember what's at stake for my role in training this girl. She is to be his and I can't mess with her. I can't get my eyes stuck on her and let my mind imagine things that simply can't be.

Marcel tries again, jerking his head at me as if with the added emphasis I would hear him. I just shake my head and shrug my shoulders, pushing one shoe off with the toe of my other foot. I hate wearing shoes. There's something about them that just irritates me. They fall to the ground and

Marcel shakes his head, reaching down to pick them up. He holds them in the air, still talking, the toothbrush bouncing up and down, then opens the dresser and dumps them into the bottom drawer. He uses hand motions to indicate that's where I should keep them in the future.

I close my eyes.

Then my headphones are ripped away.

I open one eye, then the other.

"Food," Marcel says, slowly and loudly.

"Don't fucking touch me."

"I didn't fucking touch you. I touched your headphones."

I reach for them but he holds them out of my grasp. Taking a deep breath, I close my eyes again, internally counting in order for my anger to subside.

"Food," Marcel says again. There's silence for a bit and then I hear him spit into the sink. "She needs food."

I sit bolt upright. Shit. I hadn't even thought of it.

"Kitchen," Marcel mutters at my unasked question. "Just grab anything you want."

The kitchen is small. A gas burner sits on the bench. Dirty dishes are stacked into the sink as though waiting for a maid to arrive. But the fridge and shelf that acts as a pantry are overflowing, and the freezer is packed. I open the fridge door, wondering what sort of food she likes. Then I remember that shouldn't matter, so I grab a tray covered in plastic from the back of the fridge. It looks as though someone has made a cheese platter and then decided against eating it. I wonder if it's Marcel's and then I decide I don't care. Grabbing a packet of crackers from the shelf and tipping them onto the tray, I walk down the hallway and key in the combination to her door. I'm just about to walk in when I duck into the cleaning cupboard instead, and grab a cloth, knowing I need to clean the wounds on her wrists properly.

As I walk in, I utter the command phrase. She's sitting on the bed, eyes downcast, refusing to look at me. When I get closer, her eyes lift, but only to look at the tray of food. I can almost see the hunger in her expression. Almost, but not quite because she still won't look at me. I don't know why it bothers me. It shouldn't. It should be something I'm training her to do. Look down. Show submission. But for some reason, I want her to lift those eyes.

"Come," I say, trying to soften my tone. "Kneel."

Even with her eyes still locked on the floor, I can see her battling within. I want to tell her I'm only trying to help.

"You hungry?" That makes her look at me. There's so much going on in her eyes. Hatred. Hunger. Humiliation.

I focus on her wrists. "We need to clean up those wrists." The blood has dried and the wounds are superficial, but I still need to clean them. At my words, her hands drop to her sides, the hatred in her eyes burning harder than it was before. I grab her wrist, pulling it toward me. Even if she hates me, I've still got a job to do.

"You're hurt."

And there are those eyes again. They burn into me accusingly, so I try to make her understand. I don't want to hurt her. I tell her that. And I also lie, telling her there will be no pain unless she chooses it. I feel little guilt for my lie, wanting it to bring some sort of relief, hope even, as useless as it is.

"Open."

And here goes the battle again. She sits still, frozen almost. Her muscles strain with the effort of holding herself back, but all she does is stare at the food. She doesn't reach for it, doesn't open her mouth so I can feed her. I try to tempt her, pushing the plate closer, telling her there's no point in starving herself, but her only response is to move those dark eyes back to me. She's gone from not looking at me, to staring unwaveringly, like I'm caught in an unwanted staring contest.

And then I see something I can hold over her. Something I can use as both a reward and a punishment. There are so many questions racing through her mind. So I tell her that. I tell her she's doing well. But all that gets me is more loathing in her glare.

With a heavy sigh of what I hope comes across as annoyance, I pick up the cracker. I need to set her straight. Maybe she thinks she can escape this. Maybe she thinks it is temporary. It isn't. This is to be her life. Her eyes study my face as I speak. If her not looking at me was disturbing, having her glare so unflinchingly is even worse. But at the

103

end of it all, when I command her to eat, she does.

I count it as a win. Even though she's silent. Even though she snaps the food from me as though she wishes it were my fingers, I still count it as a win.

Marcel is watching cartoons when I return. He's dressed in nothing but a tight pair of underwear. I grab a blanket from where it's fallen to the floor and toss it over him.

"Feeling a little insecure, are we?" He grabs for his dick and shakes it, laughing to himself. Then turns onto his side. "Who's Everly?"

I ignore him and fold myself onto the bed, pulling the blanket over my head.

Marcel chuckles. "You're not going to tell me? Fine. I'll just ask Junior instead."

"She's no one." I force the words from my mouth, not wanting to talk about her, not wanting someone like Marcel to know she even exists.

"And how would this no one feel, knowing you've got a hard-on for Junior's girl in there."

"It's not like that."

"What's not? That this Everly's not your girl, or that Junior's little fuck-toy in there makes you want to do bad, bad things."

"Shut the fuck up."

"A sore spot, huh? Would you want this Everly knowing what you're doing? That you get to—"

"She's my little sister," I say between gritted teeth,

unwilling to hear more of the filth he insists on spouting.

Marcel's demeanor changes instantly, and he holds his hands up, owning his error. "Sorry," he mutters.

Reaching for my headphones, I tug them over my ears, closing my eyes and attempting to block out the world with the sounds of 'Nirvana', but each time I do, Mia appears, glaring at me with all the burning intensity of hatred she can muster. I wish I knew why it bothered me so much, seeing the animosity in her eyes. I shouldn't care. But I do.

It takes around half an hour before Marcel flicks off the TV. But just when I think that I might finally be able to settle into some sort of sleep, he starts to snore. And although it isn't loud, it's irritatingly constant, even through my headphones. They are supposed to be noise canceling. They aren't.

I'm not used to sharing my life with another person, even if he is only a roommate. I'm used to silence. My own space. My own thoughts. His presence is intrusive, and I find it hard to switch off. Everly has always lived in the mansion with the rest of the family while I took up residence above the stables. Well, that was until Senior sent her away to boarding school. But not any old boarding school; it is the best school in the country and something I would have never been able to give her. In fact, they've given everything to Everly that I would have never been able to. That's why I'm resigned to this life, morbidly content to do all that Senior requests just to keep her safe and happy. If Senior is willing to give her everything I can't in exchange for my loyalty, I'm willing to give it to him.

It's around one o'clock when I finally admit defeat and get up. Tugging on my jeans, I wander down the hall and back out the door. The stairs creak as I climb them. The stables are empty of people, only the sigh or snort of a horse to break the stillness of the night.

The moon is round and full. It spills light through the windows, casting square patches of silver onto the cobbled floors. My footsteps are loud, even though my feet are bare. The horses look over at me curiously, wondering who their midnight visitor is. One of them whinnies and shakes her head, blowing hot air over my hand when I hold it out. She's got a deep chestnut coat that glimmers in the moonlight. I rub the blaze of white between her eyes, marveling at the beauty of her. Even though I've never ridden a horse, will never own one of my own, I find being around them peaceful, like everything is right with the world. But then I think of them locked behind doors and I wonder if they feel the same way.

And then I stop thinking.

It doesn't do me any good to think too deeply, to put myself in another's shoes, even if it is a horse. It takes my mind places it is better off not going. It's a survival mechanism. Stops me from wondering too much. Stops me from obsessing over a childhood I can't remember. One that only comes in flashes. One that doesn't tell me why my sister—only a toddler at the time—and I ended up, sick and starving, hiding in the stables in the city until Senior stumbled across us.

With one last stroke of her smooth flank, I turn back to the stairs that lead below. Sitting down at the monitor-laden desk, my eyes fix on her. She's sitting under the chains, staring at the window at the same moon I was only moments before. Her mouth moves as though she is singing but I don't turn up the sound. There's something so intimate about the moment, it almost feels as though I would be intruding.

And, as if my mind wants to defy my own decision of not thinking about things too deeply, I wonder who she was before. I only know her as a girl trapped in a cell. A girl to be broken. A girl to be used.

Pulling open the top drawer, I take out the file that Senior gave me. Her name is displayed in thick text on the front: Mia Abigail Cooper. Age eighteen. Brunette. Brown eyes.

Flicking open to the first page, her face stares back at me. The photo has been taken from afar. It shows her crossing a road, looking back over her shoulder and staring directly at the camera as though she knows it is there. The wind has whipped her hair over her face. Her eyes are wide and there is a faint smile on her lips. Something I am yet to see in person. Something I will probably never see.

Notes are scrawled on the page. Her life summed up in a few short sentences. Lives at home with her mother and father. Works with her parents at the bakery they own. No siblings. The rest of it is highly detailed with the places she frequents, as though someone had been stalking her for weeks.

I close the folder with a snap. That part of her life is over now. I know that better than anyone. Once you are in the grasp of the Attertons, you never leave.

CHAPTER THIRTEEN

RYKER

The sun has risen when I open the door to her cell again. With little sleep to fuel me, I use it to harden my determination. While sitting in front of the monitor last night, watching her as she dozed in and out of sleep, it dawned on me that there is only one way to help this girl. And that is to prepare her for what's to come. Train her into obedience.

She's still asleep when I take my seat. It's amazing that she can find peace here in the unknown. Peace enough to sleep. She's still propped against the wall rather than in the bed. Her skin is pale with the cold.

"Don't say a word," I command when she wakes.

She blinks a few times and for a moment I think she forgets. She looks around the room as though she is confused. Until her gaze sets on me and then it darkens.

"Come. Kneel."

She does as she's instructed, no battle behind her eyes. She tries to use the blanket to shield herself, so I rip it from her, leaving her skin prickling with cold. And there it is again. That thick fog of desire that suffocates me whenever I'm near her. I never expected to be attracted to her. I expected to feel the same way as I did while watching the girls at the auction. Numb. But instead, my heartbeat quickens and my blood thickens at the sight of her.

I tell her what to expect. Tell her to kneel in submission when I utter that command phrase. She nods. And then I use the one thing I know she wants as a weapon against her. Information.

"One question."

I know that allowing questions will not be part of Junior's plan, but Junior is not here and I am. Besides, I'm compelled to know what lies behind her eyes.

She scans my face as though waiting for me to take it back.

"Well?" I prompt.

She doesn't hesitate this time. "Why me?"

She looks at me so desperately, my heart cracks a little. She thinks this is her fault. She thinks that somehow her actions have landed her here. She is foolish. It has nothing to do with her and everything to do with him.

"You've been requested," I inform her.

She mouths the word as though her lips have never formed it before. "By who?"

This is how I can use it as a weapon. Both a reward and a punishment. In being allowed to ask one question, receiving the answer only creates more.

But Junior is not a patient man, if you can call him a man. I snap at her, getting to my feet and looming over her to remind her of her position. But it's only upon distancing myself that I can ask her to crawl.

"Excuse me?" she spits, taken back by my request.

That is my downfall. It was a request rather than a command. I take out the lash and she scrambles away as though there is escape. She cowers in the corner and I whip the lash across her shins. Tears spring to her eyes and I harden myself to them, knowing that if she doesn't learn obedience, her punishment at Junior's hands will be far worse than anything I can serve.

But she doesn't want to submit, choosing to defy me even though her chin wobbles with the strain of keeping her tears within. I slump to the chair and command her to crawl again.

Indecision and defiance dance across her eyes.

"The choice is yours," I lie.

Slowly, ever so slowly, she rocks forward, dropping to her hands and knees. She crawls toward me, eyes locked on mine and I can't help my gaze from slipping to her body. She's naked, after all. And she is glorious. She stops when she's before me and stares at me with those sullen eyes. I swallow the knot of desire that burns within. I need to leave. I can't be here, with her on her knees before me, her breasts firm and plump within my grasp, and stop the rising need to touch her.

"Are you hungry?" She doesn't answer. "Wait here." As though she could leave.

When the door closes behind me, I draw in a breath of air. Somehow the air within that room was stifling, as though there wasn't enough oxygen and my brain was starved. But I know it was just her. She is the one who sucked up all the oxygen in the room. She is the one who burns like a flame that won't go out.

Collecting fruit and a knife, I use the time to gather my thoughts. Part of me wishes I could call Senior and refuse the job. Tell him to get someone else to do it. But the thought of what someone else might do to her is the only thing that stops me. That and Everly. Her welfare is an unspoken threat. Something to keep me compliant.

When I walk back in, her eyes fix on the knife as though it is a lifeline. Something sick inside me surges at the thought of her holding it to my throat, pressing the blade and slicing as her naked body rides mine, ending this torment of conflict that has battled within, ever since I found out the truth of who the man who saved me is.

"Open," I command, harsher this time.

As I feed her, I can't help but touch her. Her lips are soft and full, they resist the pressure of my thumb and I wonder what her lips would feel like dragged across my skin. I handle her roughly, shoving my thumb into her mouth, wrapping my fingers around her neck, all the time inwardly reminding myself that she's not mine.

112

She keeps her eyes trained on me, confronting me with her humanity as I manhandle her body, trying to distance myself while still doing what Senior requires of me. I lean forward, so close I can feel the heat of her breath, daring her to look away as I palm her breast and flick my thumb over her nipple. My cock surges as visions of taking her breast in my mouth come unwantedly to mind. Leaning back in the chair, I allow a smirk to pass over my face as she studies me intently.

"What's that look supposed to mean?"

She has a burst of insanity, forgetting where she is. Who she is. Who I am. She braces for punishment, but I just can't bring myself to strike her again.

"Nothing," I mutter.

She takes each piece of fruit from me willingly. The brush of her lips on my fingers sends bolts of lust and longing into the pit of my stomach. And other places.

I need to touch her.

Telling her to stand, I remind myself it is why I'm here. It is what I need to get her used to, being touched, being used. Holding her arms above her head, I run my hands over her body and lower myself to my knees.

She is so beautiful. Perfect. She wears innocence like a cloak, but her fragrance is temptation. She deserves to be worshipped not punished. I press my lips to her stomach, pushing thoughts of what Junior will do to her out of my mind. But they keep flooding back. I keep seeing her flawless skin marred with bruises. Her eyes blank and lifeless. I would rather see hatred than that.

And then a tear falls onto my cheek, taking me out of my haze of longing. I wipe it with my thumb and bring it to my mouth. She tastes of salt and sadness.

I move away from her and she attempts to cover herself. I imagine Junior in my place. I imagine the sting of his punishment and instruct her never to cover herself.

Then I give her the only thing I can. The only thing she craves other than freedom. I allow her another question.

"Who requested me?"

I shake my head, knowing I can't give her the answer she wants. Junior has made it clear that that piece of information is his to reveal.

She swallows as though it is painful, and I turn away from her, knowing I need to leave before I press my tongue to her cheek, wanting to swallow her tears.

"Do I know him?"

I think back to what Junior said when he came to visit, how her voice spoke to his soul. He must know her, but whether she knows him is something I don't know. He could have just followed her, lurking in the shadows. He could be known to her, infiltrating her life. He could be a stranger she stumbled across. Junior knows how to put on a show when it is required of him.

"He knows you," is all I say, then I walk out the door, leaving her with more questions dancing in her eyes.

Marcel sits at the monitors, an apple in hand and chewing loudly. He's always here, always lurking. It's getting on my nerves.

"Don't you have something else to do?" I bark at him.

He smirks, bits of apple showing through his teeth as he chews and shakes his head. "Not really. Mine are all under control. Yours though…" He whistles and shakes his head again before taking another bite. "They've really dumped you in the deep end, haven't they?" He talks with his mouth full.

"They wanted to keep her away from fuckwits like you."

Marcel grins again. "Woof. Woof," he says and winks, insinuating I'm nothing more than the Attertons' guard dog. "Why don't you get her to blow you or something? You clearly need to let off some steam."

"Fuck off." I'm a man of few words.

"Are you afraid she's going to bite?" He chomps on the apple. "Take a chunk of the old pecker?" Bits of apple fall from his mouth as he speaks. "Or is there not enough of it to be worried about?"

I walk down the hallway but Marcel yells after me. "She's showering now. She looks awfully tasty all wet. It's a good thing, I guess, since she has nothing to dry herself with. You really are rather shit at this, aren't you? Did you think it would be simple? Just bark a few orders and she would fall to her knees in submission?"

Doing my best to calm my simmering anger, I walk back to the storage cupboard and yank a towel from the shelf.

"It's about more than that," Marcel continues. "You've got to anticipate their needs. Then you've got to decide whether you wish to fulfill them."

I key in the code angrily and ignore him mouthing off behind me. Sitting on the only chair in the room, I wait for her to exit the bathroom. The water stops and she walks out. Even though she hasn't been clothed since I ripped them from her, the sight of her nakedness takes my breath away. Water drips from her hair and runs down her body in rivulets.

"Don't say a word," I mumble. She drops to her knees, but only when I feign reaching for the lash in my back pocket. I toss the towel at her and tell her to dry herself, but rather than obeying my command, she wraps the towel around her shoulders and nothing more. She doesn't drop her gaze or hold her body in submission. Aware of Marcel watching, I give the command again, only this time with more conviction to my tone.

She just sits there, testing my resolve. My eyes flick to the camera as I walk behind her and whip the lash across the soles of her exposed feet. It's almost as though I can hear Marcel clapping his approval on the other side of the wall.

But still, she doesn't move. I lash again until a hiss of pain escapes her.

"Stand!" I command.

Anger starts to boil my blood. I want to yell at her, swear and tell her how much worse it would be if she had someone like Marcel here instead of me. Wrapping my arms around her I attempt to drag her to her feet, but she goes limp like a rag doll, forcing me to drag her toward the button that lowers the chains. I press it, hoping it will scare her into submission even though I won't use them. But there's no reaction. She stays limp in my arms. By now the bubbles of anger are popping over my skin, causing bursts of adrenaline to spike.

I haul her onto my lap and she finally comes to life, struggling against me as I pin her between my legs.

"Let me go!" she hisses.

"The more you fight the more it's going to hurt," I growl.

And then I strike. Her ass instantly turns red.

"Fuck you!"

Her fight both enrages and excites me and I whack her again, relishing the stinging sensation that spreads across my hand. Again and again I spank her until she sags in my lap. Anger and lust pulse through my veins. My cock strains against my jeans.

"Kneel." I take a deep breath, attempting to calm myself. "I've already told you I don't want to hurt you." That much is true. "But I will if that's what it takes." More truth. "The choice is yours." A lie.

Her eyes burn and, for a moment, the absurdity of our situation makes me want to laugh, but I hold any and all of the emotion I have within and command her to stand. Reaching out, I place my hands on her backside, tugging her toward me. Her flesh is hot from its recent punishment.

I want to turn her around so I can look at the pink tinge but instead, I pull her closer, shaking my head when she resists. The scent of her invades me as I rest my forehead against her stomach.

"You are not your own," I tell her. My lips brush over her still damp skin. I kiss her and it ignites danger.

"Repeat," I order, barely aware of what I'm saying.

I graze my teeth over her skin, nipping and tasting her. The urge to overpower and take her pushes against my chest until the pressure is almost too much. And when I look back up at her, there's no longer hatred in her expression. There's confusion. Confusion mixed with shame and a little desire.

"You will do as I command."

She's right in front of me, the scent of her driving me to insanity. I would only need to move forward a fraction and my tongue would be on her. Tasting her.

And then I do, unable to resist any longer. She's wet, sending my lust into overdrive as my tongue runs over her slit. I forget who she is. I forget who I am and become lost in her as she trembles under my attention.

She whimpers and I groan. It doesn't take long with my lust hanging so thickly in the air. She can feel it. Taste it. She knows how much I want her. Her body tenses and she shudders, pushing against me and threading her hands into my hair as she comes undone. My own release pulses with the need to be unleashed, but I ignore it, slowing my movements and drawing the last moans of ecstasy from her lips.

The guilt of what I've done only hits when I let her go and she scrambles across the floor, eager to put distance between us. So again, I resort to giving her the one thing I can. I allow her another question. But this time she does not jump at the chance. And there is no part of her that looks at me with hope.

CHAPTER FOURTEEN

RYKER

I pull up outside Mia's house and stare at the curtains covering the windows even though it's two o'clock in the afternoon. I had to escape. I couldn't watch her on the monitor, trying to wash my touch from her body. I couldn't stand Marcel's incessant chatter.

Senior had told me to keep an eye on how her family reacted to her disappearance so he won't be surprised when he checks the GSP on the car. Already the local newspaper had leaped on the story, relishing the mystery of her disappearance. Senior knew the disappearance of a local girl from a small town would create far more attention than he wanted, but Junior always got want he wanted, and in this case, he wanted Mia. Besides, they had people they could influence. The police aren't beyond their control.

I sit for an hour, maybe two, waiting for the curtains to be drawn, for someone to arrive or to leave, but the house is dead. There is only one room with the curtains open. It must be Mia's. I try to think of her sitting on the other side of the glass, staring out at the quiet street. But the vision of her huddled in the corner keeps interrupting my thoughts.

After coming to the conclusion that no one is home, I get out of the car and make my way over to the house, constantly checking to make sure no one is looking. I try the door but it is locked, so I walk around to that one window that isn't covered. Her room is warm and colored with innocence, belying her age. Her bed is messy and clothing is scattered across the floor. Posters cover the walls, but I can't read what they say due to the dirtiness of the windows.

"What are you doing?

I don't move when I hear the voice. I force a relaxed smile and turn to look at her. It's Mia's friend. The one with the pixie-style haircut. She's dressed in green.

"Sorry, I didn't mean to intrude. Is this your house?"

She doesn't return my smile. "No. But I know it's not yours."

I take a step closer, squinting from the brightness of the sun behind her. "Do you know if Mia Cooper lived here?"

Her eyes narrow. "Who are you?"

I run my hands down my jeans as though I'm nervous and then hold one out to her. She doesn't take it. "I'm a reporter with—"

"You can stop right there." She starts to walk toward the front door. "Fuck off. This is private property."

I need to keep up the façade, so I follow. "Did you know her? Was she—"

"What part of 'fuck off' did you not understand? Was it the 'fuck' or the 'off'?"

I hold up my hands. "Whoa there, young lady, I'm just trying to do my job."

"Fuck. Off." She steps toward me, repeating the words like a broken record. "Fuck. Off. Fuck. Off."

Clearly she does not share Mia's innocence. Her eyes are daggers. Her hands are clenched fists at her sides.

"I'm leaving." I walk back toward my car as she knocks on the door, throwing glances at me over her shoulder.

"Abigail, you in there? It's just me, Roxy. Let me in." The door opens a few moments later and Roxy slips inside.

I only catch a glimpse of Mia's mum, but she doesn't look well. Her skin is pale, and her eyes are sunken into her head as though she hasn't slept in years.

I decide not to go back to the stables straight away and head to visit the bar where Mia was taken. It's a quiet local bar, nothing fancy. In fact, it's in need of a good refurb. The paper is falling from the walls in places, something on the floor sticks to the soles of my shoes, and even the dart board needs replacing. There's only a couple of people here, both sitting at the slot machines, pulling on the levers time and time again and sipping on what I assume are pints of beer.

"Beer," I say and sit on one of the barstools. I don't specify a brand or a type. I don't care. It's the owner who serves me, I know this from Mia's file. It was stupidly thorough. He rips the cap off the bottle and places it on the bar before me. Condensation covers the green glass and I bring it to my lips, a sigh escaping as the cool liquid slips down my throat.

"You visiting?" The man behind the bar picks up a cloth and wipes the bench, even though it is already clean, unlike the floor. I suppose he will know everyone in town. He knows I'm not a local.

"Just here for a few days," I reply, taking another gulp.

A rugby game is playing on the TV in the corner and I twist my attention to it.

"We don't get many visitors. Not a lot going on to draw them in, you know? You visiting family or something?"

He's suspicious, wary of strangers. I guess I would be too if someone I knew had vanished into thin air right under my nose. I decide to use the same ruse I did with Roxy.

"Reporter."

The man shakes his head. "No comment."

I lift the bottle. "I just came for the beer."

"Good. I barely knew the girl."

I take another gulp, nodding my head. "And I suppose you've been inundated with people asking questions."

"Reporters. Police." He starts unloading the dishwasher behind the bar. "But it's the locals in here that are the worst. Gossip." He shakes his head, stopping midway between the bar and the shelf, glass in hand. "It's non-stop. Everyone knew her. Every now and again she would sing here, but only when someone pressured her to. She had the voice of an angel."

I lift my eyebrows, feigning the impression that this information was new to me. "Did you notice anyone hanging around or anything suspicious?" I hope it sounds like something a reporter would ask. Even though his first response was no comment, he seems keen to talk.

"If I did, I would have told the police, not some nosy reporter with nothing better to do other than sit in a bar and drink all afternoon."

I pushed too quickly, so I hold up my hand as some sort of an apology and order a whiskey instead, throwing it down my throat recklessly. I don't drink often, but when I do, I do it well. Another and another go down my throat until I can feel the numbing heat of the alcohol spreading through my head. I don't ask the man behind the bar any more questions, but I can tell he still wants to talk. He keeps starting to say something, then stops himself. I pretend not to notice. He's the sort of man who will only speak if he thinks it's not expected of him. Finally, he walks over, leaning his elbows on the bar.

"There was this guy who came in one night and he seemed transfixed with her. He was dressed all in black and just leaned against the bar for most of the night. It was a little odd, but I thought nothing of it at the time. He seemed harmless enough. And it was a few weeks before she went missing."

It was the perfect way to describe Junior. Seemed

harmless. But it's the 'seemed' part that applied to him, not the 'harmless'.

"Did you tell the police?"

"Of course I did. Gave them footage of him too." He points up at an old camera in the corner above the bar.

"It works?"

"Of course it works. I wouldn't have it there if it didn't."

For some reason I don't believe him. Instead, I order another whiskey or two, chuck them down my throat and get to my feet. After paying the bill, I thank the man and stumble out. It's only when I slide behind the wheel that it occurs to me I shouldn't be driving. So I allow myself to slouch onto the bench seat of the truck and sleep it off.

It's dark when I wake. Through the windows of the bar, I see it's a far livelier place at night than it was during the day. I imagine Mia on the stage, hand wrapped around a microphone. I wish I could have heard her sing before she was taken. Before she was frightened into silence with captivity.

Feeling sober enough to drive, I start the engine and begin the trip back to the stables. Everything is dark and silent back at Silver Oaks. The jockeys and stable hands have left for the day and nothing greets me but the gentle sigh of the horses. I run my hand over the white blaze of the chestnut mare as I pass, and make my way down the steps, stopping in front of the monitors to check on Mia. She's asleep. And this time, she's actually in the bed. She looks peaceful. It's almost as though there is a slight smile on her face. I wish I could see it for real. I wish she would turn those dark eyes on me, just for once, and see warmth, happiness. But that's not going to happen. I'm here for one reason and it's not to make her smile.

Tomorrow is a new day. I feel like some progress was made with our last training session. But then I think of the way she tasted, the way she felt, and I'm conflicted. I want to save her. Rescue her. Protect her. But I also want to slam her against the wall and devour her, plunge into her until she screams my name.

I'm no better than they are.

Marcel isn't about, so I slip into her room, careful to make as little sound as possible and kneel beside her bed. A strand of dark hair covers her face, so I push it aside with my finger and that touch alone is enough to send tendrils of lust into my core. Her lips are full and plump and her skin is pale under the moonlight streaming through the window. Flawless. It's a word Junior used to describe her. One that makes my insides shrink when I think of why he wants her so flawless.

Leaning forward, I brush my lips over her skin ever so softly and whisper her name. She doesn't wake and it strikes me as insane that she can find peace here. She doesn't grasp her situation. She doesn't understand the danger she will be in if she doesn't learn to obey.

Slipping quietly out of the room, I find Marcel standing in

nothing but his underwear, staring at the monitors. He looks at me knowingly.

"Careful there, Romeo. Owners don't like it when their guard dogs want to play with the other pets."

I push past him. I'm too tired and too drunk to deal with him. I need to do a better job. I need to demand her obedience and prepare her for what's to come.

It's the only way to help her.

So I rise early the next morning and watch her until she wakes. I use the command phrase. I order her to crawl. I touch her, steeling myself against her appeal. I tell her she must respond to my commands with a phrase of her own. But instead of complying, I'm met with defiance again. It stirs both annoyance and admiration within me. But if she does it with Junior, he will destroy her.

"Turn around," I command when she refuses to obey, yet again.

Something has changed. She's less afraid of me, of her situation. Instead of glaring at me, she faces the wall, ignoring me. Testing me.

"Turn around!" I yell, and this time it's deafening in the small space. Her shoulders are square, her chin tilted high, her ass gloriously bare. Pulling the lash from my pocket, I extend it and whip it across her flesh. A red welt appears in a perfect line across her pale cheeks. But still, she doesn't budge. She doesn't even flinch. Again and again I strike her. I know it stings, but she doesn't cry, she doesn't beg, she just stands resolutely and takes it. She's found me out. She knows my weakness. I don't want to hurt her. I'm not allowed to hurt her. This pain she's experiencing now is the worst it can get while she's under my command.

"Turn around," I say again, and this time there's a touch of pleading in my voice. She doesn't know what's at stake.

Grabbing a fistful of hair, I jerk her head backward into the crook of my neck and hiss into her ear. "Don't be stupid. You can make this stop. All you have to do is obey."

The way she ignores me lights a fire of desperation and I shove her into the wall. My cock hardens as my body is pressed against hers and I inwardly curse myself for my weakness.

"I will put you back in those chains."

It's an empty threat but she doesn't know that and her body tightens. She doesn't like the thought of being chained again. I twist her around to face me but she refuses to meet my eye. For some reason this enrages me more than anything else. I want to beg with her, plead with her to obey. Gripping her chin between my fingers, I force her to look at me. She closes her eyes. Her lips are right there. So inviting. So enticing. I push my mouth against hers angrily, no longer sure if I am doing it for him or for me. She lets her body go slack, slumping against the wall so I have to hold her up by digging my knee between her legs, almost as a seat. I take her mouth again, sucking on her bottom lip. I bite, hoping to elicit something, anything but this limp doll act.

Nothing.

"Please." There's more than just a hint of pleading this time. I'm begging. "I don't want to hurt you."

But she's leaving me little choice.

I let her go and she slumps to the floor as I walk out the door. I expect Marcel to be there, watching the monitor with a smirk of triumph on his face, but he's not. He's in the room with the blonde girl. The one he calls Star. His back is to me but I can tell he's suffocating her with his cock, his head thrown back in ecstasy as he forces her back and forth. I bang on the door. In the monitor, I see him rip her head away from him as she sits meekly at his feet.

"What?" he yells.

I push open the door as he shoves himself back into his pants.

"You could have waited," he says, folding his arms over his chest.

There's no other way to say it other than blurting it out. "I need your help."

requestor

CHAPTER FIFTEEN

REQUESTOR

The steps are wide and sweeping, a circular staircase that leads to the rooms I know I'll find my father in. They are large and grandiose, filled with all the things my father deems beautiful. Paintings so real it feels as though you could step inside their world. Antiques so old their cracks tell stories. Stuffed animals, endangered and rare, so lifelike you avoid their claws. Women so pretty they could be dolls.

One day this will all be mine. But not yet. Unfortunately, despite his age, his penchant for cigars and alcohol, the old man is as strong as an ox.

My footsteps echo loudly and laughter litters the air as I approach, punctuated with the heavy guffaws from my father. I knew he would be with them, his pretty dolls, the ones with beauty and poise but no passion or talent. Nothing but empty vessels. Clearing my throat, I wait for him to notice me standing at the entrance to his playroom. He's dressed in a thick gown, loosely tied at the waist. A glimpse of his wrinkled chest pokes through the open strip and sickens me.

"What do you want, Junior?" his voice is clipped. I hate when people call me Junior. Especially him. I despise the name. It implies that I am less, nothing more than an inferior version of my father.

He looks over at me with frustration and pushes a girl from his lap. She falls to the ground ungracefully and scrambles to her feet, fear in her eyes as she glances my way. My father is easily distracted. Easily fooled by his girls. He likes them frivolous and stupid. I do not. I am not inferior to the man. I am more.

I speak through gritted teeth, trying and failing to hide my anger. "When I visited she had wounds around her wrists. I specifically instructed she was not to be hurt."

It's the first time I've spoken to him since I made the request for my songbird. At first, I was surprised he agreed so easily. I was expecting a fight. Expecting to come up against his usual wall of refusal. But I was quick to discover there were caveats to his agreement. Someone else was to train her. Just the basics. Just enough to ensure my anger didn't get the better of me as it had in the past, but it still made me seethe that he didn't trust me. That he trusted his beloved employee more.

She is with him now and although he has my instructions, I don't truly know whether he is heeding them. It's driving me crazy. All I can think about is what he is doing to her. She's completely at his mercy when she belongs here with me, protected by a cage fit for the sweet nightingale she is.

"Ryker will do as he's told." My father's tone has softened a little, and, for a moment, I think it is to alleviate my concerns, but then I see the direction of his gaze. Lily. The flaxen-haired beauty is his favorite. Unlike the others, she's been here for as long as I can remember. She holds a special place in my father's heart and it infuriates my mother. I can tell by the set of her jaw anytime she lays eyes on the girl. Not that you can call her a girl anymore. She's older than the rest. The only one who has retained her beauty. The only one who hasn't had it stripped from her.

Crossing my arms over my chest, I level my gaze at my father. "But how do I know that?"

"Because," my father stands, stepping toward me, "Ryker has never let me down before. I only asked him because I trust him. As should you. Besides, Everly ensures his obedience."

Everly. Ryker's little sister. She was my first obsession. A pretty little thing. But my father has made it known she is off-limits, only to be used as a way to control his guard dog. But he will not be around forever. In the meantime, I will enjoy the way it makes Ryker's eyes flash whenever I mention her name. I will relish the way fury licks his skin, knowing there's nothing he can do other than contain it.

"But if you are truly concerned, he has sent a recording of her training. It's in the top drawer of my desk."

Rage pulses through me at the thought of my father's

insolence. How many times has he watched her? My songbird is for my eyes alone. The insult of having someone else train her is painful enough, but knowing my father is keeping parts of her from me starts the blood buzzing in my veins.

Buzzing of blood. The hum of electricity that pulses through me. It is a torment and an ecstasy my father will never experience. He is a simple man, obsessed with wealth and power. He does not see beyond what is right in front of him. He doesn't see past the skin to the blood that flows beneath, the lifeline, the source of passion and desire, brilliance and pain, the essence of life. No. My father is a feeble man, too easily taken with the vessel rather than the talent within. He doesn't feel things the way they are supposed to be felt. Music does not speak to his soul. Art is nothing more than pretty colors on canvas. He does not see the pain and the torture behind the skill of dance. And words are nothing but arranged letters used for the transfer of information alone.

One might not think this when looking at his collection. And indeed, his collection is beautiful. But that's all he sees when he looks at it. Beauty. The surface. The outside. The mask the world wears.

Storming from the room, I bound up the stairs, down the hallway and burst open the doors to his study. Rifling through the contents of his desk drawer, it takes a while before I find the small USB stick, insert it into his laptop and sit down on the leather chair.

The screen flickers and fades before she appears on the screen. She's sitting against the wall, knees pulled to her chest and staring at the stars out the window. The buzzing of my blood grows louder, but it's a hum of elation rather than rage. The light is dim, but somehow it only makes her more beautiful. Her mouth moves, chanting the words to some unheard song, and I fiddle with the volume controls, wanting, no—needing to hear her voice again. But the fool has recorded it without sound. I fast forward through the clip but there is nothing more, just the silence of her sitting and staring at the stars. Getting to my feet, I push the laptop off the table, not caring when it falls to the floor and smashes into pieces.

Ryker has done this to infuriate me. To break me. To ignite my anger and cause me to do something stupid, something that might make my father renege on his promise. Again. But he does not know the extent of my desire. He does not know what I am willing to suffer in order to get my songbird.

He called me a coward when I pressed my gun to his head. Said I wasn't a man. If only he knew the truth. He doesn't know that I longed to feel his throat between my fingers. That given the chance, I would smash his skull and make Everly watch, just so there was no doubt in her mind who was superior. I would make her mop up the blood that spilled from his body and then dance over his corpse.

The thought alone excites me. I take a few deep breaths, just the way I've been taught. In. Out. Inhale. Exhale. I keep going until the buzz to my blood subsides and I sink into my father's chair again, my gaze drawn out the window at the horses trotting around the track, cooling down after a hard day's training.

I think back to watching my songbird from the shadows, following her around the small town and getting to know the aspects of her life. Closing my eyes, I think of her body cutting through the water during her morning swim. There is something so inviting about seeing her skin wet. It glistens in the light, stirring lustful thoughts. I follow her home, along the familiar streets to her house. She's teaching piano to a small girl in a pretty pink dress. The little girl presses the keys to 'Hush Little Baby' while my songbird sings. I close my eyes, losing myself in the sound of her voice. Once they are done, the little girl moves away from the piano, holding out the folds of her dress and twirling. Through the window, I watch my sweet songbird smile and stroke the material. Her eyes light up and she presses her hands as a prayer beneath her chin as the little girl twirls again.

Pretty dresses for pretty girls.

I sit up.

My songbird needs her feathers.

Pulling my cell phone out of my pocket, I dial the number for my driver, my bodyguard, my Ryker, Cameron. But unlike my father with Ryker, I do not keep him close. I make him stand to the side, watch from afar, choosing not to have him obvious in my life. His presence only infuriates me.

He answers on the first ring.

"I need you to make a delivery."

mia

CHAPTER SIXTEEN

MIA

The girl falls to the ground as though she's been thrown, her elbow hitting with such force it leaves grazes of blood. Her eyes dart, taking in the bed, the camera, the chains, before coming to rest on me. There is no fear in her expression. No curiosity either. She is blank. Devoid of emotion. She scrambles to the corner, hunkering down as though I'm the one she should fear.

"Hi." The word doesn't come out right. It's too deep, too raspy, so I clear my throat and try again. "Hi," I offer.

She stays huddled in the corner, unable or unwilling to lift her eyes. Her skin is pale, gray almost. There are dirty-yellow bruises on her neck. Scabbed welts on her back. She's shivering, her whole body trembling so much I don't know if it's from fear or cold.

"What's your name?" I ask. It's such an inconsequential question under the circumstances. Names don't matter. We don't matter. But it makes me feel more normal. Whatever normal is.

Her head lifts but it's only to jerk toward the camera as if she's warning me he is listening. I pull the blanket off my bed and approach her cautiously.

"I'm Mia." I drop the blanket over her shoulders and lower myself to the ground next to her. "Are you okay? Are you hurt?"

It's a stupid question. Of course she's hurt. It's plain for anyone to see. She draws the blanket tight, wrapping it around her shoulders.

"Have you been here long? Do you know where we are?"

Again, her eyes flick to the camera. She would have been pretty once. Before the flesh left her body and she turned to skin stretched over bone. Before she was left battered and bruised and broken. Her hair could be called blonde, although straw would be a better descriptor. She has pale eyes, so pale they almost lack color. But as she glances upward, toward the camera again, I see a hint of blue.

Even under the blanket she still trembles. I reach out to rest my hand on her knee, offering her comfort but she recoils as though I have struck her.

"It's okay. I'm not going to hurt you."

Her look spells disbelief.

"I'm like you." I keep pressing, keep hoping she will talk. "They have me trapped here too."

Her eyes scour my body and, for a moment, I wish I was marked like her. Instead, apart from the redness around my wrists, and the minimal welts on my backside, my flesh is unblemished. She despises me for it. I can tell by the way she looks at me. Her gaze holds a coldness that I thought was only in the eyes of my captor.

Lifting the blanket, she raises it over her head and hides. From me, from him, from the camera, I'm not sure.

I suspect she is to be part of my punishment, but I'm not sure how. She seems fragile enough. Unlikely that we would be required to hurt each other. Unlikely that she could.

It isn't until the middle of the night that I find out their intention. I'm sleeping on the bed, blanket-less as she remains huddled in my corner. The one where I can see the stars. She isn't looking at them though. Maybe it hurts her too much. She's been here a lot longer than I have, it's plain to see in the emaciation of her face, the despair in her posture.

I don't wake to the door opening, instead, I only know they are here when a voice fills the room.

"Wake up!" It's not a voice I'm familiar with. It is someone other than my captor. Fear snakes its way into my chest and wraps around my heart. I'm disorientated for a moment. In my dreams I wasn't trapped in a room, but the reality of it all comes swooping back as the lights blink on and the girl in the corner throws the blanket off and crawls or shuffles or scrambles to the men, taking position on her knees, hands looped behind her back, head down in submission.

I lie still, too scared to move, but pretending I'm firm in

my rebellion. There are footsteps and his face crosses into my line of sight. It strikes me as strange that I don't even know his name. This man has taken me, struck me, demanded my submission and yet I have no other name to call him other than my captor.

"Don't say a word."

I squeeze my eyes shut, blocking him from my mind. Or at least attempting to. He grabs a fistful of my hair and yanks me upward, dragging me off the bed. I thrash and struggle, but the pull against my scalp hurts too much. I'm scared that if I don't follow, a clump of my hair will be left in his grasp. He releases his grip when I am beside the girl, and I fall, steadying myself with the palms of my hands. She doesn't look my way. She remains still as a statue, kneeling in submission.

I look up to meet the eyes of my captor. Rage dances in their shadows. Then my gaze slides to the man next to him and it is as though the room freezes and I half expect to see my breath coming out as puffs of mist.

The fear that is wrapped around my heart drops to the pit of my stomach, sending ripples through my entire body. The man smiles. It is evil and cold and littered with malice. But there is no tug of familiarity. If he is the one to have requested me, I do not know him.

"So, this is the one?" he sneers, bending down to examine me as one might survey discarded trash.

I hold his gaze, refusing to flinch, refusing to let him see the fear that has turned my blood cold.

"Don't say a word."

It's my captor that speaks and my eyes move between them, weighing up my options. Do I keep up my defiance and test my tolerance for pain, or do I submit? For I know it is pain that is coming. I can see it in the new man's eyes. The way they roam over my body, noting my unflawed skin. He steps forward, hand raised as though he's going to strike me, but my captor stops him.

"This is Star." My captor nods to the girl beside me. "And this is her trainer, Marcel."

So not my captor. Another trainer but one far more malicious than mine. The man called Marcel grins again and I want to hide under the blanket like Star did earlier.

"They are going to give us a demonstration in obedience as Star here has learned her lesson well."

Bile rises in my throat. I don't want to see this. I don't want to witness this girl's broken submission. Marcel steps in front of her. Close enough that the tips of his boots touch her knees.

"Stand," he commands.

Star smiles. She smiles. Not a hesitant smile. Not strained or false. She stands, uttering the words, "Yes, Master."

Marcel is face to face with her. His breath spreading over her like a fog, but she doesn't move, she doesn't flinch, she simply stands with her hands still looped behind her back, open and exposed to him.

Without warning, Marcel grips her chin with one hand and shoves the other into her mouth. She gags as his fingers hit the back of her throat and Marcel turns to my captor, a sinister grin crossing his face as he pushes his fingers deeper, causing her to convulse.

But not once does she take a step back. She doesn't twist her head. She doesn't bite his fingers. Those pale blue eyes fill with tears, but they remain steady on him, awaiting his command. Slowly he pulls his hand back, mushing his fingers over her lips and leaving trails of saliva dripping down her chin.

"On your hands and knees." The commands are said quietly with no anger, no hesitation. Her obedience is expected.

"Yes, Master." She drops instantly, turning to offer him her backside.

I want to cover my eyes. I want to hide under the bed. Anything but watch him treat her like this.

Marcel fumbles with the buckle of his belt, removing the dark leather from around his waist. The girl presses her head to the ground, tilted to the side so I can see her face, her backside jutting into the air. She knows what is coming and yet she doesn't try to escape. Her body doesn't tense. She does not brace herself.

Marcel lifts the belt and brings it down across her backside. She blinks and bites her bottom lip. He does it again. And again. And again. Tears roll down her cheeks and mine.

"Please stop," I whimper as a line of blood appears.

Her eyes widen and lock on mine. She shakes her head but the movement is so slight, I wonder if I imagined it.

"Crawl." His voice is heightened now. His body has come alive, moving and jerking excitedly, eyes dancing between Star, my captor, and me. It's almost as though he's looking for approval in my captor's eyes. But he doesn't get it. The turbulence of emotion is there behind the ocean-blue, but it's hard to decipher. It's as though his emotions are in a language separate from mine.

"Yes, Master." She crawls around the room like a dog on a leash, looking to her master for approval, for acceptance. Stopping at his feet, she awaits his command. He nudges her knees with the tip of his boot.

"Open your legs."

"Yes, Master." And she spreads her knees.

Marcel crouches so he is eye-level with the girl. He palms her breast and flicks his thumb over her nipple causing it to bead to a peak. He leans forward even further so his mouth is at her ear. "Play with yourself."

There is no shame, no delay as her hand drops. "Yes, Master."

I close my eyes. I can't watch anymore.

"Watch," my captor says.

I keep them closed, bracing myself for punishment that doesn't come. Instead, I feel his closeness as he leans over me, his lips brushing my ear just like Marcel's did to Star.

"Watch," he hisses.

When I don't open my eyes at his request, a slap sounds but it is without pain. My eyes unwillingly snap open and I see the red welt across Star's face even as she keeps rubbing circles over herself. Marcel's eyes are glued to her as his hand reaches to adjust his erection.

"Open your mouth."

"Yes, Master."

The sound of a zipper. And then he pulls himself out. His cock is large and hard. Thick veins snake their way down its length. He cups her chin as she waits expectantly for him, mouth open.

"Enough," my captor says.

My body sags with relief.

"You're going to deny me this?" Marcel's cock is in his hand, his fingers stroking up and down.

"We don't need to see any more."

Marcel laughs, tucking himself back into his jeans. "You shy, Ryker, or are you just threatened by my huge cock?"

Ryker. He has a name.

Stormy eyes narrow and he steps forward, muttering something to Marcel that wipes the grin off his face.

Star has drawn her knees back together, resuming her position of submission. Marcel walks over and strokes her face. She lifts her eyes adoringly at the touch, almost nuzzling into it.

"We shall continue our fun later, my little Star." His words are soft and threaded with affection. She smiles again and then drops her gaze when his hand leaves her.

"Your turn," he says to me.

CHAPTER SEVENTEEN

MIA

The drum of my heartbeat increases until I can hear nothing else but the pulse of my blood rushing through my veins. I close my eyes again, breathing deeply. I can do this. I can resist.

"Don't say a word." It's my captor. Ryker. His voice is a command but also a plea.

I swallow the saliva that's pooled at the bottom of my mouth and inwardly start counting. What? I'm not sure. I just chant numbers internally as if having something else to concentrate on will take me away from this place.

"Don't say a word." There is controlled anger in his tone this time. Rage bubbles just under the surface.

I know what I'm supposed to do. Kneel. Submit. Obey.

But I do nothing.

Ryker nods to Marcel and Marcel raises his hand, palm open, ready to slap Star. And that's when it hits why she has been brought here. For whatever reason, whether it be Ryker's choice or my requestor's, I am not to be damaged.

But the same rules do not apply to Star.

Her head snaps back with the impact. The redness on her cheek deepens and blood appears on her lip. It would be so easy to kneel. All I need to do is change my position, adjust the way I'm sitting. But I don't. I can't.

Marcel lifts his hand again, pausing for a moment to give me the chance to obey. I don't. More blood appears on Star's face. This time from her nose.

"Don't say a word!" The rage is obvious now as Ryker looms over me. His body trembles as though he's struggling to control himself. And in a strange moment, I laugh at the absurdity of it. A man yelling at me to not say a word while I sit without saying a word.

Something breaks within Marcel and he whacks Star over and over until she falls to the ground. Then he kicks her, his boot impacting with force into her stomach as she curls in on herself. I can't allow it any longer. The need to save her from the pain is too great.

"Stop!" I yell, crawling over to her and attempting to shield her from his rage. "Please, just stop!"

Ryker tugs me by the hair, pulling me away from the girl. "You know how to make it stop."

Marcel keeps kicking her. Again and again. She's whimpering now, crying as she clutches her stomach, folding in on herself in such a way that his next blow hits her head.

It's too much.

I can't do it.

I scramble to my knees.

"It's my pleasure to obey your command," I yell. Yet the blows keep coming. "It's my pleasure to obey your command!" I yell louder.

"Stop!" Ryker orders.

Marcel freezes, eyes wild with bloodlust. He takes a step back from the girl, running his hands through his hair as though soothing his rage. His breaths are heavy and pained. Star pulls herself off the ground and resumes her position, kneeling beside me.

"I'm so sorry," I whisper.

She doesn't acknowledge me. She keeps her eyes trained on the ground, one eye so swollen it's almost fully closed. Blood drips from her nose and stains her teeth.

Because of me.

No.

Because of them.

She holds her body so still, I wonder if she feels the pain at all.

"Crawl."

I drop to my knees, hair falling around my face and start to crawl.

"What do you say?" His voice has lost its rage.

"It's my pleasure to obey your command." I struggle but I make it sound believable, well, believable enough. I crawl in a circuit around the room, just like Star did, and come to a stop at his feet.

I am broken.

I am ashamed.

"Look at me." The command is almost a whisper.

I lift my eyes, ignoring the tears that are freely rolling down my cheeks, dreading the next words, begging him not to say them.

"Open your knees."

A sob escapes. I hesitate, looking over to Star. But she still has her eyes trained on the ground. I wonder if she's spotted the red stone.

Marcel lifts his hand and I slide my knees open, sinking closer to the ground, sinking further into despair.

And then I wait for those next words.

But they never come.

Instead, Ryker turns, nodding to Marcel. "You may leave." He jerks his head toward Star. "Take her with you."

Marcel lifts his chin at Star, indicating she should stand, and then walks over, looming above me, his dark hair falling into his eyes. He hovers like that for a while and I meet his gaze, hoping every ounce of loathing is clear in my expression.

Then he spits.

It hits my face, most of it landing on my lips and I instantly gag, spitting onto the ground, wiping my face clear. Marcel's hand raises, but Ryker stops it mid-air.

"Touch her and fucking die."

Those malice-filled eyes glare at me, scalding my skin as

they dance over every inch. He feigns coming toward me again, jerking his head as though he's about to spit, but I don't flinch. As long as Ryker's here, I'm safe from this depraved man.

Star is not.

There is no fear as she follows Marcel. She does not turn to look at me as he clips a collar around her neck. Her body jerks forward as he tugs on the lead. And then she is gone.

I cannot stop the trembling as I kneel at Ryker's feet. My teeth hurt from being clenched together. The nails of my fingers are digging so hard into my palms, I'm sure they have drawn blood.

My captor squats, balancing on his heels, elbows resting on his knees. He tilts my chin and I allow him, lifting my eyes to meet his.

"I am not Marcel. I do not wish to be Marcel. I do not want to hurt you and I certainly don't get any pleasure from inflicting pain." He tilts my chin upward again as I let my gaze fall to the ground. "The only reason I'm doing this is because I'm the only one your requestor trusts not to scar, fuck or maim you. But he does expect me to train you. He expects your obedience. He's given me a specific set of rules, guidelines if you like, and I will ensure that you learn to obey them. I won't beat you like Marcel beats Star, but I will find ways to make sure you obey."

His eyes search mine, flicking from left to right as if trying to burn in the importance of his words.

"Do you understand?"

I nod.

Ryker gets to his feet. He places a hand on my head and the heat of it burns my scalp. And then he walks out, leaving me alone with the nightmare of pain I just witnessed looping through my mind.

CHAPTER EIGHTEEN

MIA

There is no escaping this fate. I am trapped here. To be trained for pleasure and given over to a man, his to command.

I know now that there is no point in fighting it. Star's bloodied face keeps flashing in my vision as though she is still here, lying on the ground, cowering as he kicks her over and over.

I'm huddled in my corner, watching the stars. Their shine has lessened, as they remind me of her. Who was she before?

She was someone's daughter, maybe someone's sister, someone's lover and now she's stuck in a nightmare, living in a cell like mine, awaiting footsteps that are far crueler than the ones that visit me.

Ryker was right. I should be grateful.

With the nightmare on repeat in my brain, I need something to concentrate on and distract me from this reality. Every comment, every sideways glance I can remember receiving is now examined under a different light.

I am desperate for a clue, longing to figure out who requested me. Who is to become my master. But my memories give me nothing new.

Ryker continues to come to my room regularly. I smile. I obey. I crawl, open, stand, sit, kneel on command. He brings treats to my room. A pillow. A mirror for the bathroom, a plastic one. Another blanket for my bed.

There are times when I wonder if I dreamed of Star and Marcel, if they were just a figment of my imagination trying to rationalize my submission. Ryker never mentions it. In fact, he rarely talks, apart from issuing commands. And even then, there is an unspoken understanding between us, as though he wants me to know that he doesn't want to be here. He doesn't want to be doing this. But again, I wonder if I'm seeing things that simply don't exist. He may not be the one who requested me, but he is still the one who is keeping me captive, the one that demands my submission. Ensures it.

At times he is affectionate. He examines my body daily. Running his fingers over my skin and leaving it tingling in his wake. I have felt no one's touch but his since I arrived. There are times when I crave it. Just to feel the warmth of another human. Not to be alone.

He scolded me when he found the imprints in the palms of my hands, reminding me that my body doesn't belong to me. I am not allowed to blemish it. He made me chant it. Say it over and over until the words were burned into my brain.

Until they appeared in my dreams.

And now, even in sleep, he is here.

I fantasize about touching him. Imagine what his skin would feel like under my fingers. His hands are rough and calloused. Is the rest of him the same? Does the ink that shows when his sleeves slide upward cover just his arms or does it trail across his body in an array of color?

What would he taste like?

I no longer feel shame when he brings me to climax with his tongue or fingers. Instead, I look straight into those stormy eyes, so he knows how I feel, so he sees my release, the only pleasure I have left to feel.

I reached out for him once, unable to control myself. I was rewarded with a sharp sting across the soles of my feet and a stern warning never to do it again. But despite my recent lesson in obedience and submission, it only made me want to touch him more.

He is forbidden.

And yet I know there are times when he wants to let me. Times when his eyes roll to the back of his head and his jaw clenches as though he's fighting against some force that threatens to overwhelm him.

I shower often, letting the scalding water turn my skin red. It runs over my face, drips off my nose and falls to the floor, swirling around the drain before disappearing. I wonder where it goes. Why it hesitates. If I had a drain I could crawl down, I would in an instant. I wonder what it gets to see. I miss my daily routine. I miss drowning out the world underwater. A shower is as close as I get.

When I turn around he is watching. He leans against the wall, arms and ankles crossed. As soon as I turn, he pulls himself straight, but I still catch the glint in his eye. The lick of desire.

This man is the one who brings me to a trembling mess with the stroke of his tongue. He is the one who commands me. Who knows every inch of my body. Who feeds me. Who controls me.

And yet, he is doing this for another man. A man he will not name despite me asking every time he allows me a question. He terrifies and excites me. The sound of his voice gives me comfort. Any emotion in his eyes causes my chest to swell as though I am proud.

And I hate myself for it.

"Come here." He jerks his head, pulling the towel from the railing.

I pad over to him. Ever obedient. Ever submissive. I consider kneeling but he hasn't said the command phrase. I am not expected to be in full submission mode yet.

Wrapping the towel around my shoulders, he dries my body as I stand still. The towel is soft and if I close my eyes, I can imagine I am in the embrace of my lover. Someone who cares.

I lift my arms, bend my legs, turn when he needs me to. Once he is done, he folds the towel back over the railing.

"Follow me." He turns and walks out of the bathroom. I follow. "He's allowing you to be clothed."

Sure enough, a rack of clothing now stands at the foot of my bed. But it is not filled with jeans and t-shirts like I used to wear, it is filled with silky dresses and lacy underwear. All in shades of reds and black. Soft reds that remind me of the blush of a rose. Bright reds that make me think of the lipstick Roxy likes to wear. And deep reds that remind me of blood. I run my fingers over the material longingly. I have been naked for so long, I no longer care. No longer feel shame.

Because my body is not mine. It is his. Whoever he is.

"Pick something. Get dressed."

The dresses call to me. Apart from the red stone, the shampoo and body wash, my world is gray. I pick a dress made of a material that slides over my body and hugs my hips. I am still naked beneath it and my nipples form peaks due to the coldness of the material. It feels like ice but looks like fire.

His eyes watch me appreciatively and a spark of boldness ignites within me. Maybe it's because I'm clothed. Maybe it's because I feel less of something and more of someone.

I walk over to where he is leaning with one shoulder propped against the wall and stand so close I can see waves of the storm in his eyes, each hair that covers his chin, each line that mars his forehead.

Slowly I lift my hand. It shakes as my fingers spread,

inching toward him. I search for permission in his eyes but find only conflict. War. A battle.

I am so close, my fingers only a whisper away from touching him. I hold my breath. I think he's holding his. And then his hand flies upward and he grips my wrist like a vice. There are bloodied scrapes over his knuckles that weren't there before.

"Don't touch me."

"Why?" I whisper, our faces dangerously close.

"Because you're not mine."

"And yet you touch me."

"He's allowed me to. It would be hard to train you if I wasn't."

"Who is he?"

His eyes are still locked on mine. "You know I can't answer that."

I swallow. It's painful. "Why me?" My voice is barely audible, afraid of breaking this spell between us.

"You've already asked that."

"But what did I do to make someone think they can own me?"

He shakes his head as his eyes scan my face. They fall to my mouth and he swallows, his voice coming out soft and tender and broken.

"It has nothing to do with what you have or haven't done. It is about him. It's because of who he is. Not who you are. You are merely something he wants."

Then something changes in his expression. He remembers where we are, who he is, what he is supposed to do. Pain shoots up my arm as he twists my wrist viciously.

"Don't say a word," he growls.

And I fall to my knees, the spell broken.

CHAPTER NINETEEN

MIA

I wake with fear prickling my skin. Something is wrong. I can feel it. I'm taken back to the first time I woke here. The panic. The dread. The terror.

But my wrists are no longer chained. There is no blindfold covering my eyes. I am lying in bed, the only light coming from the moon shining through the square patch of a window. It's full tonight. Full and bright. From the amount of times I've seen it move across the sky, I've been in this hellhole for at least ten days, but it seems a lot longer. It's as though the Mia of before, the one who laughed and smiled and sang, is from a different lifetime, one that seems disconnected from this one.

My heart thuds loudly, though I don't know why. Something has woken me. I just don't know what.

I lie still, my ears straining to make sense of why I'm awake. I can't make out anything in the dim light, most of the room is shrouded in darkness.

And then someone clears their throat.

And it's not Ryker.

I know Ryker's voice. I know the sound of his breath, the noises of his body.

"Hello?" I call out cautiously.

No one answers but I can hear breathing now. I wish there was a light to turn on, something to expose my fear, but the switch is on the other side of the door. The side I've never been on.

I search the darkness. There is no red light on the camera.

"Ryker?" My voice is timid, scared. But I know it's not him. Has my requestor come to visit? Am I about to come face to face with the monster who haunts my nightmares?

Sitting up in the bed, I keep the blanket wrapped around me. I have sleepwear now, satin chemises with lace that cup my breasts.

The sound of footfall jerks my head to the corner where Ryker often sits and Marcel steps into the patch light. His gaze is predatory. His smile is vile. His nose is swollen as though it's been hit.

"What's the phrase he uses? Keep quiet? Say nothing?" He steps closer and I freeze, perched on the edge of the bed. In another place, in another life, Marcel would be considered handsome. But not here. Not now. The smirk that covers his face paralyzes me with terror.

"What do you want?" My voice is small in the darkness.

Images of Star's bloodied face pulse on repeat, as though she is here and someone is turning the light on and off. It is blinding.

He steps so close I have to crane my head to look at him. But I'm determined to keep his gaze, determined not to let my fear show.

Bold in my stupidity.

"What is it about you that's so special?" He inspects me slowly, taking in my hair, my eyes, lips, chest. "I don't see anything."

I wish that were true.

"Ryker will kill you if you touch me."

He chuckles. "Is that what you think?"

I swallow the nervous knot of fear. "It's what he said."

Reaching out, his hand brushes my cheek, sending sickening surges of nausea through me.

"And how will he know? You've already noticed the camera is off. What's to stop me from doing anything I want, right here, right now?"

My voice wavers, almost a whisper. "He will know."

He shrugs and strolls around the room, fingers feathering my clothing.

"Oh," he says, "now I remember." He turns to look at me, his eyes darken, his voice lowers and evil drips from his lips. "Don't say a word." He pauses, waiting for my response, my obedience.

I do nothing.

He starts to pace again. "I see," he muses. "Like that, are we?" He sits on the bed, resting his hand on my knee.

I want to vomit.

"You're trembling," he says. And then he leans in close, his mouth brushing against my hair. "I'm going to have fun playing with you. But just remember, how hard we play, how much you suffer is up to you."

Why do they keep insisting I have choice? Does it make them feel better about what they are to do? Does it make them feel as though I'm partly to blame, that I'm asking for it?

He gets to his feet again, undoing the buckle of his belt and sliding it out through the loops.

"Don't say a word."

I stay put. My body strains with the effort. I've become conditioned to obeying, but I've become conditioned to obeying Ryker.

His hand snakes out so quickly I don't notice until he hits me across the face. My head flings to the side. I taste blood. Still trembling, I hold myself in that position, breathing deeply before turning my eyes to him, leaning forward and spitting blood onto the ground.

He lifts his eyebrows. The lines that crease his forehead aren't as deep as Ryker's but somehow, they are harsher, more sinister. And then he hits me again. Harder. Hard enough so I fall to the bed. He climbs on top of me, pinning my arms to the side of my body with his knees. His hands claw at the material of my slip, pulling at the lace until it rips. He tears it away from my body, but I don't scream.

I don't know why I don't.

Maybe it's because I know no one can hear.

Maybe it's because I'm frozen with fear.

Maybe it's because there's no point.

His hands are on me and I close my eyes, wishing for escape as he roughly explores my upper body. His hands are cold and smooth and clammy with excitement as he massages my breasts between his fingers, occasionally pinching my nipples painfully. He smiles when I wince and lowers his head, his tongue, thick and wide, leaving cold trails of moisture across my chest.

Grunts and groans cut the silence. He grabs my chin, jerking my mouth open. "Don't get your hopes up," he growls. "I'm not stupid enough to put my cock in there." He spits and it hits the back of my throat. I gag, but I can't move, pinned to the bed by the weight of his body. Again and again I gag, desperate to remove his fluid from my mouth before it slides down my throat.

But it is useless.

My body convulses with the effort of trying to remove him. He grins down at me, his hands threading into my hair and tugging sharply.

"Careful," he pants as I gag once more. "You're getting me excited."

Then he leans close and I'm covered in the stench of him. He smells of savage cruelty, rotten flesh and putrid blood.

"And you don't want to get me excited, my little petal. I

lose control when I get too excited."

The bed bounces when he gets off, but his hand is still twisted in my hair. He tugs and I fall. I kick and lash out as he hauls me across the floor and over to the corner with the chains. He yanks them and they fall noisily, clattering to the concrete.

"No," I plead, eyes wide, head shaking violently, ignoring the pain it brings with his fingers still knotted in my hair.

"It's too late for that. I told you how hard we played was up to you. I gave you the chance to obey, to make this pleasant." His lips curl on the word. "But you refused. Now I get to do things my way."

Hard metal clamps around my wrists. Marcel leaves me slumped on the ground and walks over to press the button that lifts the chains back into the cavity in the ceiling. I have no choice but to get to my feet or be dragged. Higher and higher he raises the chains until I'm stretched on my tiptoes.

I start to scream.

He cuffs my throat, blocking off my air and my cries. "Scream all you want. No one can hear you. These walls are soundproof, or didn't you know that? This place has been specifically built. You see, the man who has requested you, it's his family business. Well, one of them anyway. They trade in women. Steal them. Break them. Train them. Sell them."

He speaks loudly to be heard over my strangled screams. But they are diminishing with each breath whistled through

166

vocal cords stretched too tight.

"But not you. You are special. You are chosen," he hisses, releasing his grip under my chin. He sighs heavily when I keep screaming. My throat is raw, the pressure of where his fingers dug into me burns, but I don't stop. It's my only hope.

"Enough!" he orders, stepping behind me. My screams turn to a strangled cry when his fingers wrap around my throat again. This time he squeezes hard. Hard enough to cut off the air, hard enough that panic slices into my gut. I can't claw at him. I can't fight. I'm at his mercy. Or lack thereof.

"See?" he breathes into my ear when my screams stop. "Isn't that better? So much quieter."

He doesn't release his grip.

This is it.

I'm going to die.

Desperation to breathe gives me enough energy to twist in my restraints, a last-ditch effort for air. Darkness swirls in my vision, creeping in the sides, leaving nothing but a hole that is filled with the square patch of moonlight.

And then his hand is gone, and I suck in air, choking and spluttering as it fills my lungs and coats my raw throat. He walks slowly over to the bed, retrieving his discarded belt. It's then that I notice the studs of silver that dot it. Small but vicious.

"Now you are going to learn what happens when you don't submit."

The pain of the lash is nothing compared to the bite of his belt. I can't help the cry of pain that escapes. There is no point pretending I'm strong anymore. Defiance has deserted me. Moisture beads on the skin of my backside. Blood. Small droplets that rise from the broken skin.

I am alone with the devil.

Six times his belt scorches my skin. Across my backside, my thighs, my back. The pain is almost unbearable. I say almost because I know there is more to come. I know it because of Star. I know it from his grunts of depraved desire.

Metal clinks against concrete. He has dropped his belt. But it does not bring comfort. There are things worse than his belt. His heavy breathing scares me. It's not from exertion. It's from excitement.

When his body presses against mine, it is no longer clothed. His hard cock pushes against my backside, slick and sliding with my blood. His hands travel over my breast, twisting my nipples sharply.

I'm crying. I hadn't noticed before but my cheeks are wet with tears and my vision is blurred.

"Please," I beg.

"Please, what?" he asks, his tongue reaching out to lap my neck.

"Please stop."

"Did you do as I asked when I asked nicely?" His hands travel down my body, over my stomach. My breath hitches when he reaches the bone of my hip. "No. You didn't."

His cock pulses. His fingers snake further. And then they are inside me. It's too much. I need to escape. I can't be present. But there is no relief as he pushes, animalistic moans grunted into my ear as he rubs his body against mine.

"You like that, don't you?" He pushes further, twisting his body to allow him deeper access. "Yes. I can tell you do. You just wait until it's my cock inside you. I will take you. All of you. It's what's supposed to happen. It's how you are supposed to be trained." He groans, his tongue once again lapping my skin, tasting the cold sweat that covers my body. "Ryker thinks he can keep you all to himself. Well, that's not the way it works around here. Sluts submit. To everyone."

The words are only just out of his mouth when the door bursts open and Ryker storms across the room, ripping him away from me. He knocks him to the ground, pinning him with his body, and throws punch after punch into his face. Marcel yells. He screams.

It is a beautiful symphony.

Marcel tries to cower from Ryker's onslaught but there is nowhere to hide. Ryker is relentless. His fists pound into flesh over and over until exhaustion is the only thing that stops him. Getting to his feet, he draws in a breath heavily, wiping the spit from his mouth with the back of his hand.

"You're done here." His voice is colder than ice. Walking over to the door, he holds it open and jerks his head at Marcel. "Get out before I change my mind."

He can barely stand, but somehow Marcel makes it to his

feet, blood dripping from his face, eyes swollen, nose broken, body naked. He stumbles out without a glance in my direction.

CHAPTER TWENTY

MIA

Relief slumps my body just before the pain engulfs me. And then Ryker is there, lowering the chains, unlocking my wrists and gently lifting me into his arms.

He is warm.

He is safe.

My head falls to his shoulder as he carries me to the bathroom and turns on the shower. I waver in and out of awareness, not wanting to face the reality of my existence. His hand hovers back and forth under the stream of water. His arm is bare, the tattoos on his skin dark. He steps forward and the water washes over me, causing me to wince.

But I am still in his arms.

I am still safe.

How long we stand there, I'm not sure. Shielded in his embrace, my hands looped around his neck, clinging to him, water pours over us. It is tinged red when it swirls around the drain, stained by my blood.

I study the dark ink on his arms. I see four stars, dotted

into a cross. I've seen them before, out the square patch of window. I don't want to think about the pain. I don't want to think about who inflicted it. My hand falls over his skin, slick with water as I trace the lines of the stars on his shoulder, the pattern forming a diamond over and over, the perfect distraction from all the thoughts I don't want to think.

His eyes are on me, but he doesn't say a word. He just stands with me in his arms, water falling down our bodies. With the side of my head pressed to his chest, the sound of his heart echoes, slowing the beat of my own until it matches his. I close my eyes, concentrating on nothing but the gentle thud.

When he lowers my feet to the ground, I tighten my grip, wincing as pain slices through me once again. In his arms, it had numbed, but now it is back in force. Gently, he turns me, allowing the extent of my injuries to show. When he first touches my wounds, I let out a cry or a sob, covering my face with my hands.

His touch is gentle, washing away the blood. I brace myself against the wall, needing strength more than my own to keep standing.

The water stops with a clunk. He pats me dry. Even the threads of the towel hurt as they brush over my skin. And then he lifts me again, one arm hooked under my knees, carefully avoiding the welts on my thighs, the other cradling my back, unable to evade the broken flesh. The wounds are not deep, they will heal without scars, but the memory of his touch will forever be with me.

I shiver even though I'm not cold as he lowers me to the bed. The absence of him cuts me, and I reach out, needing to be close to him. Close to safety. To familiarity. To the only thing I can cling to. But he disappears back into the bathroom, wet footprints left in his wake.

I don't want to be alone. I can't be alone. I don't want to close my eyes and see his face, his evil smile and depraved desire as his belt licked my skin. My throat throbs where his fingers dug into me. My flesh is on fire, hot and burning, stinging with flames of torment.

Through the opening of the bathroom door, I can see him peeling the singlet from his body. Both arms, both shoulders are covered in tattoos. Sleeves of art. They are all black. They snake over him, moving with the muscles that slide under his skin. His jeans are the next to be torn from him, left as a wet mess on the floor. After rubbing the towel over his body, his face and his head, he wraps it around his waist.

He still hasn't said anything but when he walks back to me his eyes say more than words ever could. Pulling back the covers, he crawls into the bed and lies down on his side, his forehead pressed to mine, face to face. He doesn't offer apologies or excuses. He knows they would be meaningless. Reaching out, he draws my hands away from where they are clutched to my chest and holds them between his, bringing them to his lips, pressing soft kisses over them.

There is something different in his touch. Something gentle. Something filled with remorse and longing. I shuffle closer, needing his warmth, and my body tenses with pain. He lowers our joined hands, giving me space to bend my head and press it to his chest. I need to feel the beat of his heart again. I need it to echo mine because my body is so cold inside, I don't know if my heart is still beating. His knees bump against mine and thread between them. The towel is gone and his body radiates heat. I need that warmth. I crave it. If I could pull back his skin and climb inside, I would.

I'm not sure how long it is before my body stops trembling and my heart starts beating on its own. I tilt my head back, hesitantly looking at him. It's the first time I've touched him. The first time he has touched me when I've longed for it. The grooves in his forehead are deep, etched with unease. Summoning my strength, I lift my hands and smooth them out. His eyes bore into mine, saying all the things words can't. I press the lines of his forehead over and over, frustrated that I can't remove the depth of them. Reaching up, he pulls my hands away, encasing them in his own again. He breathes deeply and his head inches across the pillow. His features blur with closeness and his lips press to mine, breathing warmth back into my body. He presses a kiss to where the skin is split. He presses another to the tightness of my cheekbone. Another to my nose.

I start to cry and he captures my tears with his tongue.

Then his hand threads into my hair and tugs my head to his chest, allowing me to keep my tears. My cries turn to sobs, racking my body in pain again.

Ryker just holds me, his hand twisted in my hair, my head pressed to his chest, our legs tangled together in a mess of flesh and limbs.

I cry until there are no tears left.

I cry to exhaustion.

For a moment, when I wake, I am transported back to the knife of fear before Marcel stepped out of the shadows. My heart beats rapidly. Cold sweat coats my skin.

But then I feel him.

He is still here.

His hand is still cupped around the back of my head.

I'm still breathing into his chest.

I can still feel the steady thud of his heart.

Everything about this man is confusing. His softness—the way he touches me so gently, cradles me as though he's scared I might break—is a contradiction to his sternness. Here, now, he isn't the man who's kept me locked away in this hellhole. It's almost as though he abhors it.

I draw in a ragged breath. "Why?" I whisper.

He doesn't answer for a long while. I think he might not answer at all, and then words rumble in his chest so low they could almost be mistaken for a growl.

"Because I..." his voice falls away. "Because I have no

choice."

He didn't need to ask what I meant. He already knew.

Why is he doing this?

Why has he locked me in a cell, imprisoned me?

And why is he showing me kindness now?

"No choice," I repeat. "There is always a choice. No one can take that away from you."

They were the same words he had uttered to me and they aren't lost on him. He shifts a little in the bed, moving his large frame around my body, somehow engulfing me further. He clears his throat as though dislodging something painful and draws in a ragged breath.

"I don't remember much from my childhood. I don't remember my life, day to day, my mother, my father. There are parts that come in flashes, bits, but none of them make sense. They're more of a dream than a memory. No recollections of events or the moments leading up to them, they are just there. But the memories of living on the street are more vivid. The hunger. The desperation. I don't know why I was there. I don't know if I ran away or if I was abandoned. But that's when I met him, the father of the man who has requested you. He found me hiding in a stable, buried beneath the hay, delirious with fever."

The rumble of his voice is comforting, the vibration of his voice against my cheek, the movement of his chin against my head.

"He..." He swallows. "He rescued me. He took me in,

gave me a job and protected the one thing that means the most to me. He looks after the people who are loyal to him. He's been more of a parent to me than my own."

I take advantage of the crack in his wall, pressing him for more details of his life, wanting to know what makes the man holding me who he is. "You don't remember anything of your mother?"

My mother and I have always been close, a special bond that I know nothing can replace. It breaks my heart to know he never got to experience it.

Pressing the tips of my fingers to his chest, I wait in silence, not wanting my voice to break the moment. His skin is warm and firm. His fragrance intoxicating. His words, his warmth, and his scent take me away, alleviating the pain and crushing the walls that surround us, transporting me to his past.

I willingly dive into the escape.

"I'm not sure, I barely remember anything about her…" He pauses. His body tenses as though talking about her causes him physical pain and I wonder what must have happened to him to make his tone so cold, so empty.

"I have these memories of a smile, of whispered words spoken against my scalp, but I'm not sure if I'm remembering her, the sound of her voice, the way she looked or if it's just another woman that was part of my childhood. It's like my memories have been blocked, barring any recollection of her from my mind."

"So nothing?" I just want him to keep talking.

He swallows and the sound is loud. "I have these flashes. They're kind of like photos in my head, ones where the world is frozen but I can move around them like some sort of suspended dream. The most vivid one is of opening a door to a room that she was in. I don't know where I was before, in a house, our house, someone else's, but the curtains weren't pulled properly and there was this light that shone across where she lay on a bed, illumining her face like a halo. I don't know if it was the sun, or a streetlight or something else entirely. The door creaked as I pressed it open and walked across the floor. I had to be careful not to step on any of the stuff that was scattered across the carpet. I can't recall what it was. Clothing or bottles or pizza boxes. Just rubbish. But there was this stain in the shape of a heart. Sort of. It was cracked open like someone had grabbed the two sides and just yanked."

His voice takes on a trance-like tone, one laced with nostalgia and pain. I'm transported to that room with him. Closing my eyes, I imagine the light coming in through the window, the scattered mess and the stain on the floor.

"I remember sort of poking her, testing to see if she was awake. Her body jiggled but she didn't open her eyes. It's strange, but I remember all this, the scene of whatever it is, but I don't remember what she looks like. I don't remember if she had blonde hair or brown, if her eyes were blue or green or gray. I must have pulled the curtains because the halo of light was cut off, and it took a while for my eyes to adjust. Mascara was smeared under her eyes. Lipstick had fallen lopsidedly off her mouth. There was an imprinted red mark on her cheek. And there was blood but for some reason, it didn't shock me. I just remember thinking she was beautiful. Everything is so vivid in this memory, but ask me what our daily lives were like, where we lived, what people we were around, and I couldn't tell you. I just remember this desperate need to protect…" He falls silent, the only sound I can hear is the thud of his heart and the flow of his breath.

"So do you think it was after that you were out on the streets?"

Ryker lets out a steady stream of air. "I don't know. I don't know what made me leave, if I chose to leave, if she forced me, or if I had no other choice. I remember hiding in the hay and making a bed for…" His voice trails off again.

He's hiding something. A part of his life he doesn't want me to know.

"But I remember everything after. I remember Senior taking me back to his place. I remember stuffing myself with food, of sleeping in a bed that felt like it had come down from heaven."

"Senior?" I question, locking onto the name.

"That's what I call him."

He doesn't offer any more of an explanation and I don't push. Somehow, I know it would be pointless. Taking a deep breath, he increases the grip on the back of my head, drawing strength from me instead of the other way around. His next words come out quickly, as though they are painful as they pass through his throat and he needs them gone before they burn.

"I owe him. He saved me. That's why I do the things I do. That's why I'm here with you."

I lie still, hoping he keeps talking. His heart beats faster now, but it is still steady and unbroken. I can feel the muscles of his jaw working back and forth, as though he's contemplating what to say next.

"They are my family, in a way. As fucked up as it sounds, they're the only family I've ever known, or at least that I can remember." He inhales deeply and searches in the darkness for my hand, threading his fingers through mine, the other hand locked in my hair. "That's why."

I tilt my chin, so my lips brush over his chest as I speak. It seems easier to talk without his eyes on me. "Marcel said that this is their family business. They trade in women."

"It's not everything they do. They are more than that."

"So it's your business too?"

He pulls back then, moving his head far enough away so he can look me in the eye. They are flecked with all the colors of an ocean storm. Gray. Blue. Green and silver.

"Yes," he whispers. He's waiting for my reaction. Waiting for the judgment in my eyes. "No," he changes his mind. "Maybe. I've never done this before, never trained someone. This isn't what I would choose." His eyes dance between mine as if begging me to understand.

But I don't. "That doesn't make it okay."

His body tenses and he moves away a fraction. "I owe him everything. I owe him my life."

"But you don't owe him mine."

"It's not just me." He speaks so quietly, I can barely make out the words. "I have a sister I need to look after too."

This is the part he was hiding from me. "Where is she?"

"She's away at boarding school, something I could never afford to provide her."

"I suppose she's part of the reason you're doing this. You need to provide for her and trading in women must pay well."

The bed jostles, sending stabs of pain through me as he sits on the edge, his hands pushing into his hair. "Don't say that."

"I'm sorry." Sarcasm laces my tone. "Do you prefer the term human trafficker?"

"It's not that simple. You don't understand. You haven't lived my life. You don't know what's at stake."

"And you haven't lived mine. The one that was taken from me. The one that is battered and bruised from the bite of Marcel's belt."

"I would never hurt you like that."

"But it only happened because I am here. In my life before, he would never have even known me. I wouldn't have been trapped in an inescapable room. There wouldn't have been chains for him to hold me. How would you feel if they were doing this to your sister? Would you sit still and say you couldn't let her go?"

Ryker gets to his feet, flashing the image of his pale backside. He picks up the towel from the floor to wrap around his waist again.

"You think I'm enjoying this?" He runs his hands through his hair, blowing out a long and low exhale of breath. "If I didn't do it, if I wasn't here, then someone like Marcel would be. Is that what you want? To be beaten into submission?" His eyes flash anger. "So I slapped your ass a few times. It was nothing compared to what Marcel did, right? You had a few raised welts, not the wounds that are there now. And Marcel only came in here because you pushed things. You tested me and I had to do something."

I glare at him angrily. "By allowing Star to be beaten?"

"No." His voice is thunderous. "By allowing you to see what your training could be like. None of this would have happened if you just did what you were told."

"So this is my fault?"

He takes in a deep breath, trying to calm himself. "You knew the stakes." He's glaring at me, frustration tainting his movements. And then something softens within him and he sits on the edge of the bed again, reaching out to rest his hand on my shoulder. "It kills me to see you like this."

Propping myself up on my elbow, I attempt to sit but fail when the pain stops me. "Then let me go," I plead. "Open that door. Set me free."

He gets up from the bed and paces the room, muscles flexing with each frustrated movement. He is beautiful, even now. The lines of his body are perfectly cut, as if God was paying extra attention when he made him. I want to hate him, despise him for what he has done, but at the same time he is my only source of comfort. My only hope.

"I can't." He strides toward the door.

"Ryker!" I call.

But he doesn't turn back. He doesn't hesitate. He rips open the door and leaves. A few moments later the red light on the camera blinks back on.

ryker

CHAPTER TWENTY-ONE

RYKER

Marcel's plan for enforcing Mia's obedience is brilliant, not that I'd admit it to him. But it's not easy to watch. Marcel gets a sick pleasure out of hurting the girl. You can see it in the gleam of his eye, the way his tongue darts over his lips, the undeniable smirk on his face.

I'm not sure whether to be impressed or disgusted by his training skills. Star is flawlessly obedient. There's not one fraction of hesitation, not a flinch or a whimper. She's accepted her fate.

Even though I've seen the girls before, I've never seen a display like this. I don't know what the appeal is to complete obedience, the lifeless eyes, and the forced submission, but Marcel clearly gets his kicks from it. He has no shame. It's hard to watch. But I stop him when he takes his dick out. I don't need to see that. I don't want to see that. The whole thing sits uncomfortably with me but seeing the horror in Mia's eyes makes me hopeful that I am getting through to her, that she will see what could be happening to her and chooses to obey rather than suffer like this girl is.

After Marcel's display of Star's obedience, I walk toward Mia, inwardly begging her to listen, to do what's best for us all. She's sitting on the ground where I dragged her, but her stance is anything but submissive. She closes her eyes as I approach, taking in deep breaths as though, if she concentrates hard enough, she can will herself away from here.

If only it were that easy.

"Don't say a word," I issue the command. She's supposed to change her position to kneel, hands on lap, eyes on the ground. She knows this. She's done it many times before.

But she doesn't this time.

I swallow the frustration at the back of my throat and try again. "Don't say a word."

It's a strange feeling, waiting for her to obey. Part of me is incensed that she is willingly choosing to make a simple thing so difficult. Part of me is enthralled that she's got the fire within her to defy.

I know it won't last though. She was too gentle with Star when we threw her in there. Too concerned. There is no way she is going to sit there and watch once I give the go-ahead to Marcel.

I nod to him and he lifts his hand, slapping Star across the face for Mia's disobedience. He hits her hard. Blood appears. I watch Mia curiously. She is trembling, but she doesn't move. Marcel's hand wavers in the air, waiting for Mia to submit, but she doesn't. She's willing to see this girl suffer rather than kneel. Marcel strikes. More blood.

"Don't say a word!" My anger is hard to control now. All she needs to do is kneel. It's not a lot to ask. It's not something that will cause her any pain, but still she refuses.

Marcel strikes the girl again and again. She falls to the ground and he starts to kick her. Even I have to control myself from stopping him as he strikes her again and again. It's sickening. And the thought that this brings him pleasure makes me hate him even more. The girl is huddled over herself on the ground, silent tears falling down her face. The only noise in the small cell is Marcel's grunts and the blows of his boot.

My fists are clenched at my sides. My teeth grind together until my jaw aches. And then finally Mia launches herself toward the girl, shielding her with her own body, begging for Marcel to stop.

I almost sink to the floor with relief. But she still hasn't done what was asked of her so I drag her away. She watches as Marcel continues to strike the girl, two, three more blows and then she gets to her knees, assuming the position and yelling the words she's supposed to.

"It's my pleasure to obey your command!" Her voice echoes off the walls, but Marcel has gone to a different place. He strikes the girl again and again, lost to all else going on around him.

"It's my pleasure to obey your command!" she yells again, this time looking directly at me, her eyes wide, begging me to stop this insanity.

It's only when I yell at Marcel that he ceases. His chest heaves with exertion and when he looks over at me, there's excitement in his eyes. No wonder Senior said he was one of his most effective trainers. He gets pleasure out of it. Too much pleasure.

"Crawl." The anger has gone from my commands, but she obeys without hesitation. She crawls. She opens her knees.

She looks at me and there's fear and repulsion in her eyes.

"You may leave," I say to Marcel.

But before he does, he wanders over to Mia and my body tenses. He's expressed his desire for her before. Just to piss off Junior. I'm ready as he looms over her, waiting for him to reach out and touch her. It will give me the excuse I need.

But instead of touching, he spits. I restrain myself as my hand itches to grab him by the throat and push him against the wall. He threatens to hit her, and despite the words that come out of my mouth, part of me wants him to do it just so I have a reason to react. But he knows better than to push me.

Once they are gone, I squat down to look Mia in the eye. She stares at the ground so I tilt her chin upward.

I hope she can see the honesty in my eyes. I hope she can see the pleading and the importance. She will not escape this. The Attertons are too powerful for it to be a possibility.

They know everything about her and the people she loves. There is no scenario in which she could simply walk away. And because of Everly, there is no way I could allow it.

All the defiance has left her glare. She looks at me but it's like she looks through me. Like she's not there.

From then on she is obedient. Submissive. Everything I ask of her she does without hesitation. It's hard to watch. The fire in her eyes has gone and instead there's this emptiness. She stares at me blankly when I issue a command. Her words are without emotion. To reward her compliance, I bring in little comforts. A mirror for the wall. An extra blanket for the bed. She smiles when she gets them, but it's nothing more than a muscle movement. It doesn't reach her eyes.

I examine her body daily, getting her used to touch. Used to someone running their hands over her, taking what they want, but it's like performing an autopsy. She shows no shame in being naked anymore and stops trying to cover herself. I find myself often staring at her, scared that when she catches me, she will see the longing in my eyes. But my gaze doesn't seem to affect her. She takes pleasure where she can, but in no way gives the impression that it has anything to do with me.

Until now.

Her skin is cold, only the hairs that prickle under my touch giving me any indication that she's aware of me. Goosebumps rise in the wake of my touch. It only happens when I touch her gently, trailing a single finger across her flesh so delicately it is as though I'm only touching the idea of her. And then it happens. She forgets herself and the smallest of moans escapes. Her hands are stretched above her head, her back pressed to the cold concrete wall. I've pulled the chair over so I'm seated in front of her, my head level with her chest. The nipples of her breasts are beaded and dark and sensitive. And when I run my tongue over one, it happens again. I'm not sure if it's a moan or a sigh. But whatever it is, it affects me in the deepest parts of my being. My hands are on her sides and I move them to grip her backside, digging my fingers into her flesh painfully to remind both of us where we are. Who we are. Her eyes snap open when I reach between her legs and brush one finger over her sex. She watches me as I stroke her. It's the only time she's looked me in the eye without me demanding it. It's the only time I've seen her and not the blank wall she puts between us. Not a look of despair, of hopelessness.

It's like she wants me to see her.

When I bend to taste her, her legs part ever so slightly. I inhale, letting her scent invade me at the same time as steeling myself against it. And for once, stupidly, I allow myself to imagine that she is here willingly. That she craves the stroke of my tongue and the touch of my hands. I imagine that instead of being shoved against the wall, hands kept under my command above her head, she reaches out for me, running her fingers through my hair, tugging sharply when the waves of arousal overwhelm her.

I know every inch of her body. Every reaction to my attention. It is how I know she is close to climax. She lifts onto her toes ever so slightly as though she is both wanting me closer and trying to escape at the same time. There's a quiver to her skin. A tightening. Without distancing myself from her, I run my eyes up and over her body, latching onto her gaze just as I know she is about to be overwhelmed. For a moment she forgets again. She forgets she is a girl in a cell and I am the man that keeps her trapped. We are nothing but two people lost in lust. Her hands fall to my shoulders, nails digging into my skin.

I jerk away from her, scared of what her touch will do to me. Of what it will make me want to do to her.

"Don't," I warn. And she looks at me with such longing in her eyes, there's nothing left for me to do but leave.

Before I crack.

Before I submit.

Storming into my shared bedroom, I punch the wall repeatedly, not caring when the skin breaks and blood appears on my knuckles.

I've worked for Mr Atterton for years, and in that time I've been asked to do a lot of things. Everything I did without hesitation. Everything without regret or torment.

I've stolen and betrayed at his command.

I've beaten men and left them in a bloodied mess.

I've killed and buried their bodies in the dirt.

But I've never been this conflicted.

Never this tormented.

Her gaze haunts my dreams.

The memory of her touch consumes me.

But the only way I can save her is to train her for another man to ruin.

CHAPTER TWENTY-TWO

RYKER

I'm lying in bed, headphones on and attempting to ignore Marcel. He's standing in nothing but a towel, running a piece of floss between his teeth, occasionally reaching up to flick through the channels. He stops when it shows the camera outside, a strange van pulling into the driveway. I can tell from the make and model that it's someone who works for the Attertons. The vehicle stops, and a man dressed all in black, almost a replica of me, gets out of the driver's seat.

"You know him?" Marcel asks, floss left dangling from his mouth.

The man walks to the rear of the vehicle and pulls open the door. He struggles with something, having a difficult time pulling it out of the back. It's only when the man turns, that I see who it is.

"Yup," I reply to Marcel, enjoying the way my lack of details pisses him off. I walk into the hallway and Marcel follows.

"Who is he?" he asks.

"Cameron."

"Cameron who?"

"I don't know his last name." I'm at the door now and pull it open, waiting for Cameron to appear. He's another guard with the Attertons. One assigned to Junior.

Marcel groans and rolls his eyes. "Do you enjoy being a fuckwit?"

"Most of the time."

Cameron walks into sight, tugging a rack full of clothing behind him. "Delivery for Ryker?" He grins and claps me on the back.

"Delivery boy now, are you?"

"Thinking of becoming a personal shopper. Want to be my first client? I've brought some outfits along for you to try. Anything take your fancy?" He looks along the row of clothing, picking out a silken dress. "I hope you like red."

I cuff him over the back of the head and grab the front of the rack, helping him maneuver it down the stairs.

"What happened to your face?" I ask, noting the scratches that line his cheek.

He rolls his eyes. "I got attacked by a cat." He chuckles, not even trying to hide his lie.

As soon as we stop, Marcel barges in front of Cameron, holding out his hand, chest puffed.

"Marcel." He states his name as though it means something. "I'm in charge here."

Cameron looks between us, a smirk on his face. He lifts a questioning brow my way but doesn't address Marcel's claim.

"Cameron." He states his name with equal importance. "Junior's bodyguard."

"Ah," Marcel says. "So we've got two dogs in the kennel today."

Cameron's smirk instantly vanishes and he takes a step toward Marcel. "What did you just call me?"

"Now you've done it, Marcel. Cameron doesn't have my delightful temperament. I'd watch myself if I were you."

Marcel laughs but shifts his gaze nervously over to Cameron while taking a step back. "It was a joke," he says warily. "A bit of a thing between Ryker and me. Bodyguard. Guard dog." Cameron just continues to glare at him. "I meant no harm, dude. Relax."

"Dude?" Cameron growls.

I lean in and talk low into Marcel's ear. "He hates being called dude."

Like me, Cameron is not a small man. Marcel cringes under his glare until finally Cameron breaks into a smile and whacks him on the back. "Just messing with you." He nods to the clothing rack. "Where do you want this?"

"Just leave it there," I say. "So he's decided she's allowed clothing, I take it?"

"Apparently so." He runs his hands over the materials, leaving them swaying in his wake before turning back to me with a wicked grin. "Do I get to see her or what?"

I hide my annoyance and jerk my head over to the monitors, pulling out a chair for him. Mia's in the shower. Again. She has a lot of showers. She stands under the water until her skin is pink with the heat, trying to wash the filth of this place, the filth of me, from her skin.

I don't blame her.

She despises me.

I despise me too.

Her back is to us, the water running over her head and flattening her dark hair over her shoulder blades. It isn't until she turns around that Cameron lets out a low whistle.

"Fuck," he says reverently.

Marcel chuckles. "No wonder he had to steal her, right? There's no way she'd go for him otherwise. He's as dull as a doorknob."

"You'd be surprised," Cameron says. "The dude—" he exaggerates the word "—is attractive. He's got that 'fuck-me-because-I'm-a-rich-entitled-prick' look going on. Girls seem to like that. He certainly doesn't lack for choice. They fall all over him in fact. They have no fucking clue what he's really like. He wears a mask well."

"You been busy?" I ask, changing the subject so I don't have to think about who Junior really is.

Cameron swivels in the chair. "Not really. Been quiet since he's become obsessed with her. I feel more like a nanny than a bodyguard. You? Are you having fun here?"

I flick my eyes to the screen. "I'm not sure if fun is the

right word."

Marcel laughs. "Only because he's not allowed to taste the goods. Fuck that."

Cameron ignores him and gets to his feet. "As much as I'd love to stay and chat," he winks, "I've got more errands to run. The excitement is near killing me." He claps me on the back. "Behave yourself."

"Oh, don't you worry," Marcel says. "He's being a good dog."

He grins but neither of us return it.

"Joke." He holds up his hands. "It was a joke. Maybe next time you could deliver Ryker here a sense of humor," he yells as Cameron climbs the steps.

I shove past him to grab the clothing rack and push it into Mia's cell. She's still in the shower. The water must be cold by now. The bathroom is thick with steam but I can still see her through the fog. The way the water caresses her body. The way her skin gleams as though someone has doused her in glitter. She catches me watching and I shift uncomfortably. My mask wasn't in place.

"Come here." I want to say it as a command, but it doesn't come out that way. I wonder if she hears the longing in my voice. The conflict that constantly rages within.

Ever obedient, she walks over and I dry her, running the towel over her body and trying not to think about all the things I want to do, to say. Once dry, she follows me into the cell.

"He's allowing you to be clothed."

Even though she tries to hide it, excitement shows in her eyes. She runs her hands over the clothing and I have to swallow the knot of desire as my mind automatically imagines what it would feel like for her to touch me that way.

"Pick something. Get dressed."

She chooses a simple red dress. One which hugs her frame perfectly. And suddenly she is no longer a girl in a cell. Wearing the dress, covering her nakedness, it makes her less of a thing and more of a person. She must see it in my eyes because she steps toward me with a boldness that's never been there before. She steps closer and closer until she is only a breath away. She scans my face with those dark eyes and my heart starts racing in a way I haven't felt in a long time. In fact, I'm not sure if it's ever raced this way before. Her hand lifts as she searches for permission in my gaze. And I want to give it to her. I want her to touch me, to run her hands over my skin. To want me. But if I let her, I know I won't be able to resist.

I sway with indecision. She's so close. It would be so easy.

She wants me.

But before the fire can be lit, I grab her wrist and twist it away. "Don't touch me." It's more of a plea than anything else.

"Why?" There's confusion in those big eyes.

"Because you're not mine."

"And yet you touch me."

"He's allowed me to. It would be hard to train you if I wasn't."

"Who is he?" There's the question again. The one that's constantly behind her eyes.

"You know I can't answer that."

She keeps those dark eyes trained on me in such a way that I don't know how much longer I can resist.

"Why me?" Another question she's already asked.

Her mouth is so close. I can't help but let my gaze keep slipping to her lips, imagining how it would feel if she closed the breath of a gap between us and pressed them to mine.

"It has nothing to do with you, or what you have or haven't done. It's about him, who he is, not who you are. You are merely something he wants."

I want to touch her. I want to tell her that I will take her away from all this. I want to make her mine. But I can't. It's not why I'm here.

I twist her wrist again and say the words I have learned to hate.

"Don't say a word."

Our session is quick. She does everything I command her to do, but I don't touch her this time. I can't.

Marcel is watching the monitor when I leave. Watching her. Watching me with her.

"You should just fuck her."

I ignore him and head into the kitchen. I hid a bottle of

whiskey in here the other day and I need it now. Desperately. But he follows.

"I won't tell Daddy's Boy if you do. You don't need to worry about that."

The bottle isn't where I left it.

"I can tell by the way you look at her, the way you touch her that you want her. She can tell too." He pauses. Marcel never pauses. I look up at him and see the whiskey bottle dangling from his fingers. "You looking for this?" The liquid is half gone. "You know we're not allowed it, don't you? Senior worries that we'll get too rough on the girls if we get drunk." He scoffs and takes a swig. "Too rough. Is there such a thing?"

"Give it here." I'm seething by this stage but Marcel either doesn't notice or doesn't care.

"Say please," he mocks.

He smirks and I snap, storming toward him and ramming him against the wall, my arm cutting across his throat.

"Please," I hiss in his face. It takes all my willpower not to hit him. With one final warning glare, I rip the bottle out of his grasp and walk out the door.

Marcel chuckles. "Good boy."

And that does it.

Turning quickly, I land one sharp punch straight to his nose, sending him reeling back against the wall, blood dripping.

"Stay," I order and walk into the bedroom, slamming the

door behind me.

I drink myself into oblivion. I can't stop thinking about her, so close, so tempting. The way she smelled. The way she looked at me. The way her hand trembled as she lifted it, wanting to touch. The fear that flashed across her eyes when I twisted her away. Everything within me has been so tightly wound since I came here. A constant battle.

I take a swig straight from the bottle, shaking my head as the liquid burns my throat. Walking over to the screen, I flick it on. She is trying on some of the other dresses, popping into the bathroom each time to check out her reflection. Her fingers brush over the material delicately and I have to close my eyes a moment to stop myself from imagining they are mine.

I take another swig from the bottle. Another and another. She's moved from the dresses to the lingerie. She pulls one from the rack. It's black and lacy with fishnet stockings. She sort of laughs as she looks at it, then shrugs and starts to pull it on. Beginning with the underpants, she threads them over her legs and pulls them up to slip over her hips. My cock hardens instantly. Then she takes the bra, sliding the straps over her shoulders and reaching behind to do up the hooks. Not having a lot of material, the bra only serves to accentuate what she naturally has, pushing her breasts fuller, rounder.

I groan and adjust myself, the constraint of my jeans making my erection almost painful. Turning her back to the camera, she threads one leg at a time through the fishnet stockings. The cheeks of her ass are exposed in the thong. I undo the buttons of my jeans, reaching in to release myself. Due to days of denial in the face of temptation, I'm fucking hard as steel. After taking another swig from the bottle, I begin to stroke myself, too drunk at this stage to care if Marcel walks in or not.

The final thing she does is reach down and pull on a pair of high heeled black shoes. And then she begins to walk around the room, her eyes flicking toward the camera as though she knows I'm watching.

I pump my fist, the need to come rising quickly as she stops in front of the camera. She stares directly into the lens as she lifts a hand and holds it at her neck before letting it fall ever so slowly down her body. Her fingers trail over her breasts and stomach and I close my eyes for a moment, imagining the fingers are mine. Imagining that I'm lying on the ground as she stomps a high heel over my chest. Imagining her eyes looking up at me as she takes me in her mouth.

It only takes one more glance at her to finish me. I shoot my load into a towel and immediately feel disgusted. I don't know who I've become. This isn't who I am, some disgusting pervert that wanks himself off to the image of a girl trapped in a room.

Draining the last of the whiskey into my throat, I toss onto my side, facing the wall and pull the blanket over my head, leaving Mia still staring at me through the lens of the camera.

CHAPTER TWENTY-THREE

RYKER

I wake in the dead of the night. There is no light. No sound. The TV screen has been turned off but I don't hear Marcel's snores. I'm still partially drunk when I get to my feet and have to reach for the wall to steady myself. I stumble down the hall to find Mia's monitor blank, the screen showing nothing but darkness.

Fear rolls as waves of nausea and it sobers me instantly. Racing across to her cell, I rip the door open.

Marcel is there.

He has her in chains, arms stretched above her head and he's wrapped around her from behind, his fingers plunged inside.

I see red. Nothing but red. It's like my vision is stained with it and all I want is blood. I tear him away and toss him to the ground. His eyes are wide with shock and terror as he cowers below me. I lose count of how many times I drive my fist into his face. He tries to shield himself, covering his face with his hands but it doesn't stop me. His body is covered in blood, but it's not his, it's hers. Punch after punch my knuckles hit bone. I'm not striking hard enough to do any serious damage, but enough to rough up his pretty face. Enough to vent some of the rage inside me. I don't know what it is that makes me stop, probably the thought of what Senior would do if I killed him without permission, but eventually, I pull myself away, getting to my feet and leaving him as a bloodied pulp.

"You're done here," I spit out the words. "Get out before I change my mind."

He tries to stand but stumbles and crashes to the ground, pathetic whimpers falling from his mouth. I just watch as he struggles, a sick satisfaction settling in my veins. It isn't until he leaves that I allow myself to look at her. Tears are streaming down her face, cheeks red from where he slapped her. I lower the chains, but it isn't until I step behind her that I see the wounds on her back. He's broken flesh. Deep welts are already beginning to turn purple. They cover her back, her backside and her thighs.

How could I let this happen? If I wasn't so pissed, if I hadn't drunk so much, would I have known earlier? Could I have stopped him?

I'm careful when I lift her into my arms, trying not to touch the open wounds, trying not to inflict her with any more pain. Her head slumps against my shoulder. Her arms cling to my neck as I test the temperature before stepping into the shower. Blood washes from her as soon as she's under the water.

I want to kill him.

I want him to suffer for what he's done.

As if needing a distraction, her hands trace the patterns of the tattoos that cover my shoulders and chest. Her touch is light. Hesitant. It ignites my body, sending sensations of arousal through every cell. Even like this, even battered and bruised, she is the most beautiful thing I've ever seen.

Lowering her to her feet, I keep a steady hold on her as I clean her wounds. She flinches from the pain, but she doesn't pull away. She allows me to pat her dry and lift her back into my arms.

The guilt is heavy.

She hasn't spoken and neither have I, but her eyes have said more than her words ever could. They're filled with need. She reaches for me when I lower her to the bed, scared that I'm leaving her alone. But my clothes are wet and she needs warmth. I peel them from my skin and dry myself with the same towel I dried her, ignoring the stains of blood and keeping them hidden as I wrap the towel around my waist. Returning to the bed, I lower myself beside her, face to face, reaching out to take her hands in mine, covering them, protecting them and pressing kisses to her cold skin. She's shivering. Her entire body trembles.

I want to take her pain away.

I want to take her away.

She shuffles closer, bracing herself for the pain of

movement. Bending her head, she presses it to my chest. I thread my bare legs through hers, hoping to lend her my warmth, wanting more than anything to tell her how fucking sorry I am.

She stays like that, her breath hitting my chest with each exhale until she pulls away from me, dark eyes peering into mine. When she reaches for me, I don't stop her.

I can't stop her.

She has torn away my skin and left me bare and exposed. Right now she could do anything to me and I would accept it willingly. She could plunge a knife into my heart and I would utter my thanks. She could command me to kneel and I would fall at her feet. She could threaten to chain me and I would lift my hands willingly.

But all she does is try to smooth the lines from my forehead. Her thumb presses my skin over and over as if she can erase them. Tears form in her eyes, and I pull her hands away, taking them in mine and watching her over the space of the pillow. There's such need in her gaze. Such longing. I inch closer and press my lips to hers faintly, brushing over her pain.

The tears fall then and I lick them, wanting to take away the hurt, drinking her tears as my own. Her tears turn to sobs and I pull her close, wanting to shield her from this world. From Marcel. From Junior. Maybe even from me.

It is with her head pressed to my chest that she falls into a sleep of exhaustion. Her body jerks, reliving her attack as a nightmare. I do nothing but hold her.

I only know she's awake from the change in her breathing. I'm scared she'll reel away from me. Remember who I am. Instead, she pulls in a breath and says a single word.

"Why?"

I don't need to ask what she means. I know it from the tone of her voice, from the pleading and the confusion.

Why am I doing this?

There is really only one answer I can give. The truth. The truth that no one else but the Attertons know. The truth of my past.

So I open my mouth and bare my soul.

I tell her about the flashes of memories from my childhood. The glimpses of my past that make no sense. I tell her of life on the streets, the hunger and the pain. And then I tell her how Senior saved me. Gave me a new life. A new family. A new purpose. I tell her I owe him my life. But I don't tell her of my sister. It seems too cruel to burden her with the knowledge that her captivity ensures the freedom of another.

It hurts when she asks about my mother, but I tell her the truth. The truth that I've never told anyone, not even Everly.

When she speaks again, her lips brush over my chest and send tendrils of something soft and tender into my gut. "Marcel said that this is their family business. That they trade in women."

"It's not everything they do. They are more than that."

"So it's your business too?"

I pull back so I can look into her eye, pleading with her to understand. "No. I've never done this before. This isn't what I would choose."

"That doesn't make it okay."

It's impossible to make her understand my loyalty. To make her understand that the man who ruined her life is the one who saved mine.

"I owe him everything. I owe him my life." My words are truth and lies. A perfect contradiction, just like my relationship with the Attertons. I love them and hate them. I love them for everything they've done for me, for Everly, but I hate them for everything they've made me do.

Her next words are so quiet I barely hear them. "But you don't owe him mine."

It's then that the truth tumbles from me, desperate for her understanding. "It's not just me. I have a sister I need to look after too."

She whispers. "Where is she?"

"She's away at boarding school. Something I could never afford on my own."

"I suppose she's part of the reason you're doing this." Coldness creeps into her tone. "You need to provide for her and trading in women must pay well."

I sit up in the bed, distancing myself from her before I end up doing something we both regret.

Before I beg her to forgive me.

Before I press my lips to hers hungrily.

"It's not that simple," I say. "You don't understand. You haven't lived my life." That much is true. She hasn't been exposed to what I have. She hasn't doubted she would live to see the age of sixteen. She hasn't wished for death as Senior ripped my innocence away and replaced it with something damaged and broken.

"And you haven't lived mine," she says. "The one that was taken from me. The one that is battered and bruised with the bite of Marcel's belt."

"I would never hurt you like that."

But she keeps going, insisting that none of this would have happened if I wasn't the one to keep her here. She is right. And it kills me. But there is nothing I can do. Senior wouldn't hesitate to destroy me if I betray him. I am nothing without loyalty. Marcel's right. I'm a guard dog, there's no purpose to my being without a master. I would be beaten and discarded. But that's not what scares me. What scares me is what they would do to her, what they would do to Everly. Once the Attertons want you there is no stopping them. People are nothing more than things. Things to be bought, traded and sold.

So I try to get through to her. To make her understand that I'm doing everything I can within the bounds of my power.

"It kills me to see you like this," I say.

"Then let me go. Open that door and set me free."

If only it were that simple. For a moment I consider telling her the truth of how powerful the Attertons are. Of how far their reach extends. How it's not just her in danger but everyone and everything she loves, everything I love, if I let her go.

Instead, I just say, "I can't," as I stride toward the door.

"Ryker!" she calls, her voice filled with desperation and need.

It's the first time she's said my name.

CHAPTER TWENTY-FOUR

RYKER

Senior answers on the first ring. "How is everything going? I see you had a nice time at the bar the other day. Racked up quite the expense tab."

I clear my throat, unsure how he's going to respond to the news. I'm sitting at the monitors, watching Mia as she lies on the bed, unable to remove my gaze from the dark marks on her body. Her eyes dart around the room in fear as though she thinks Marcel is coming back to finish the job.

I get up and start to walk toward the stairs, away from listening ears. "Something has happened."

Senior laughs as music plays in the background, the faint tinkling of fingers on ivory. "Something good, I hope."

"Not exactly." I'm outside, standing in the sun and I take a deep breath of air, hoping the freshness will wash away some of the tightness in my chest.

"I'm a busy man, Ryker, you know that better than anyone. Get to the point." Senior knows I'm not one to usually skate around the issue, so already he's on edge.

"She's been hurt." A horse and jockey race past, the horse's footsteps thundering over the ground.

"How?" A door closes and the music in the background fades.

"Marcel."

"Spit it out, Ryker." He is getting frustrated. "Tell me everything."

And so I do.

Senior stays quiet on the other end of the line as I talk. Occasionally he grunts or lets out a frustrated exhale of air, and when he speaks, his words are short and clipped, almost whispered. "How long will it take for her wounds to heal?"

"A few weeks before they're gone completely, I'd say."

"Fuck," Senior curses. "So he's going to find out."

"There's no way around it. Her skin is broken and the bruising has started to appear. Junior's going to know the moment he sees her."

Senior gets distracted, barking at someone in the background. I watch as the horse who was racing around the track slows, the jockey leaning forward to pat its neck, rewarding it for a job well done.

"I'll deal with Junior," he says, but he's still distracted by the ruckus of yelling in the background. "I've got to go," he says. "But I'll call you back."

"What about Marcel?" I ask.

"He's a good trainer, would be a pity to lose him. Let me think on it and we'll talk later."

It's hours before he calls again. Hours where I just stare at Mia on the screen, wishing there was some way I could go back and undo all of this.

Senior's voice is gruff and straight to the point. "I'll need you to take care of Marcel. Let him know that he's no longer required."

"You want me to let him go?"

"Affirmative."

Getting fired by the Attertons isn't what it seems. People like Marcel, like me, the people that know the ins and outs of the less public aspects of their business don't get fired. They simply disappear.

"I've got a doctor on the way to check out the girl, and I'll send someone to replace Marcel in a few days. Are you able to handle things until then? Take over the training?"

I swallow. "Sure."

And then he's gone, already distracted by the next issue that demands his attention.

Walking over to my car, I pop the boot and rummage until I find what I need. Tucking it into the belt of my jeans, I glance up once more at the blue sky before heading back below. A cursory look at the monitors tells me that Mia is right where I left her, lying on the bed, eyes still wide and scanning the room.

Marcel is in the bathroom, the odd hiss of air escaping through gritted teeth as he cleans his wounds. I walk over and lean in the doorway. His face is a mess. One eye is completely swollen shut. The skin over his cheekbone is split to the bone. His nose is crooked and his lips bulge unevenly. He's managed to pull on some underwear, but other than that he is naked.

He catches a glimpse of me out of the corner of his good eye. "Fucking traitor," he says, although his voice is distorted due to his injuries. "Trainers are supposed to have each other's backs."

"I'm not a trainer."

"And yet you're fucking training a girl, go figure."

"You know she wasn't to be touched. I warned you."

"Typical." Marcel attempts to grin but his lips only twitch awkwardly. "So what? You going to beat me some more now? Stick up for the honor of your girl?" He nods in the direction of Mia's room, turning around and leaning against the bathroom counter to face me.

His face looks like something out of a horror movie. I must have struck him harder than I thought. Clenching my fists at my sides, I test them for tenderness. Sure enough, the skin over my knuckles screams in protest.

"I'm supposed to let you go." It's only at those words that the true horror of his situation dawns on him.

"You fucking told?" He advances toward me but stops and clutches his side. "You fucking told?" he repeats.

I know I'm supposed to feel guilt. But I don't. I've trained within myself an ability to simply not think. Follow orders.

Obey. Do as I'm told. But this is one case that I don't need to block off my thoughts. Visions of him wrapped around her, fingers pushing inside, the look of terror on her face, flash through my mind. This is the one time that thinking about what I'm doing and why helps.

I stalk toward him, ramming my elbow against his throat, and push him into the shower cubical. He flails, grabbing onto the edges, stopping me from pushing him in fully, but his grip is weak and I dislodge it easily.

"Ryker," he hisses, the air in his lungs trapped by the pressure of my grip. "Ry—"

Slipping the knife from my belt, I push it into his side and jerk it upward. My name fades on his lips and turns to a low howl of air. He looks at me, shock displaying over his features as the blood starts to drip down my fist. He slumps forward, his head resting on my shoulder like an embrace.

"I said you would fucking die if you touched her," I whisper in his ear. "I'm a man of my word." Then I push him away, sliding his body off the knife and allowing him to flop to the ground.

He sits there staring, the only movement the occasional blink of his eyes until his body convulses one last time and he doesn't blink again.

Pulling the shower curtain closed, I wash the blood from my hands. It is done.

requestor

CHAPTER TWENTY-FIVE

REQUESTOR

Music is what takes me away from the vapid existence that is my life. It transports me to another world. A world filled with temptation and promise, with desire and torment, passion and pain.

The ivory keys beckon to me as I sit at the grand piano, the sole piece of furniture in the vast expanse of what my mother refers to as the music room. My father's office is down the hall and, just as I'm about to press my fingers to the keys, he walks past, his phone ringing. The brutish sound of the ringtone infuriates me, so I breathe in and out, calming myself, and close my eyes, bringing the image of my songbird illuminated by the light of the moon to mind.

Darkness descends and the world fades as I press the first key. I am alone with her. Trapped in a halo of moonlight. She lays across my piano, intricate knots of twine holding her in place, a silken blood-red dress spilling around her, ripped and torn to expose her pale body. The scarlet shimmers on the dark ink of the piano. In my vision, a breeze floats over her and ruffles the folds of silk. Her exposed nipples peak. Sweat glistens on her skin. She is bare and open for me, her eyes locked on mine.

There is only one piece to play in this moment. There is no escaping the beauty of the haunting melancholy of Beethoven's 'Moonlight Sonata'. It flows from me effortlessly, my fingers skimming over the notes of the piano without thought. I play it slower than I've been taught, slower than the music would dictate.

I want to stay in this moment with my songbird forever.

But my father's vacuous voice as he paces back and forth seeps into my awareness, ripping apart my reverie. I attempt to ignore him, but he makes no attempt to lower his voice as he answers call after call.

Breathing deeply, I do my best to block him out and lose myself in the music. And I'm successful for a time. Successful enough to be soothed by the rhythm of the sonata, at least for a while. But then his words reach me and destroy that peace, even though he has moved into his office.

"I'm a busy man, Ryker, you know that better than anyone. Get to the point."

My fingers move mechanically, knowing the notes by muscle memory as I let thoughts of my sweet songbird slip away and concentrate on the sound of his voice.

"How?" he asks as he closes the door.

I stop playing, lifting myself from the piano and walking to the door of his office, pressing my ear against the wood.

"Spit it out, Ryker." His voice is laced with frustration. "Tell me everything."

There's silence and I test the door, only to find it locked.

"How long will it take for her wounds to heal?"

Wounds? My blood spikes, rage rippling through me. Grabbing the handles of the doors, I shake them violently.

"Father!" I bellow. "Let me in!"

"Wait. I'll speak to you in a minute," he yells through the door.

The buzzing of my blood almost deafens me, making it impossible to hear as my father continues to speak to Ryker about my songbird.

My sweet, sweet songbird.

Mine.

Not his.

Not Ryker's.

Mine.

Keep reading for a sneak peek of

Until You're Mine

part two in the Requested Trilogy.

ACKNOWLEDGMENTS

Thank you for venturing along this journey to the dark side with me. I can't wait for you to read what is in store for Mia and Ryker over the next two books. Their story started out as only one book but the more I wrote, the more of their story I needed to tell.

More often than not, I lock myself away in my office, not revealing to anyone what I'm writing about and losing myself in the story until the first draft is done. Then comes the team of people I am so grateful for.

My alpha reader who gets the first glimpse of my stories and whose feedback on the plot is invaluable.

My incredible editor who makes me laugh with the comments she leaves in the margins of each manuscript.

My beta readers whose eagle-eyes and observations add those last tiny details which make all the difference.

And finally, the last step in the process, to you, the readers. Every copy bought, every posted comment, every review left and every email sent mean the world to me.

Thank you for your support.

SABRE

KEEP UP TO DATE

If you'd like to keep up to date with news regarding my books, please sign up for my newsletter:

www.subscribepage.com/sabreroseauthor

You can also find me on social media:

www.facebook.com/sabreroseauthor

www.twitter.com/sabreroseauthor

Website:

www.sabreroseauthor.com

Email:

sabreroseauthor@gmail.com

THE STORY CONTINUES . . .

Taken. Broken. Captive.

There used to be a small amount of safety

within the walls of my cell.

Not anymore.

Now my body is broken and bruised.

And he doesn't come to comfort me.

I ache for him.

His face dominates my dreams.

His body dominates my desire.

Then he offers himself to me and I lose myself in him.

But I do not love him.

I cannot love him.

To do so would risk my chance at escape.

UNTIL YOU'RE MINE

MIA

There used to be a small amount of safety within the four walls of my cell. But not anymore.

I still know everything it contains. I know every rough patch on the floor and the exact location of the red pebble. I can find it by feel. I tested myself once, on my hands and knees, fingers searching the floor until I was confident that the red pebble lay beneath.

I know the arc of the sun and the moon and how the square of light will spill across the room, over the floor, and the shape of its distortion when it touches the walls.

I know the stars that travel across the sky, not their names but their patterns, the ones that blink on and off. But I no longer think God is watching. It would be too cruel if He were.

I know the level of shampoo left in the bottle. I know how far to twist the faucet to stop it from dripping. I know the shape of the watermarks that stain the walls.

But now it seems foreign. It no longer feels safe. I watch the red light of the camera, knowing that if it flicks off my nightmare might begin again.

There is nothing to tell what is beyond that door, whether it leads to more doors, just like mine, or if Star and I are the only ones here. Or if she is here at all.

I haven't strayed from the bed since Ryker left. I'm lying in patches of blood that have seeped into the sheets from each time I shift. My entire body pulses with pain. I cannot escape it. I can feel every lash of Marcel's belt across my skin, and each time I swallow, the pain is a reminder of his fingers around my throat.

I long for relief, for Ryker to come back and hold me in his arms, or at least to give me a painkiller. My prayers are answered when the beeps of the keypad sound and the door sighs open. But the face that rounds the corner isn't that of Ryker's. Instantly, I recoil from the stranger, but when Ryker walks in behind him, my racing heart calms.

"Ah, yes." The man walks over and kneels beside my bed, placing a case down on the floor and opening it to peruse its contents. "What was used, may I ask?"

He talks to Ryker and not me. In fact, the man doesn't look me in the eye at all. His gaze floats over my body then back at the case lying on the floor. Ryker hasn't looked at me either. It's like his eyes are glued to the man at my side, as though there's some magnet that keeps his gaze away from me.

"Leather belt," Ryker says. His eyes flick my way, just once, and so quickly that had I not been staring at him, I wouldn't have noticed at all. "Studded," he adds. He swallows and his Adam's apple bobs up and down in his throat.

The man kneeling on the floor draws in a whistle of air and shakes his head. He's rifling through the contents of his case. His glasses keep slipping down his nose. I lean further over on the bed, wincing at the pain it brings, but manage to see what's in his case. He must be a doctor of some sort. I allow myself a small smile when I see the collection of pills and potions in his case, desperately hoping that he will give me something to relieve the pain.

"Is she allergic to anything?" Again, the doctor looks to Ryker for the answer.

Ryker shakes his head, this time his eyes caught on the ground. "Not according to her file."

The doctor nods and tips a couple of pills from a pottle into his hand. "She'll need water," he says to Ryker.

As Ryker leaves, I beg him to look at me. I need to see into his eyes. I need to know what he is thinking, why he won't look at me. But he doesn't even give me a backward glance.

The doctor instructs me to lie on my stomach as he examines my wounds. He makes tutting noises and shakes his head, but he doesn't speak to me. When Ryker walks back in, the doctor takes the glass of water from him and tells me to take the pills. Even with the water, they are painful as they slide down my throat, but I don't begrudge the pain as I know it will bring relief.

Ryker leans against the wall behind me, out of my line of sight as the doctor continues. He draws blood. He takes swabs. He listens to my heart and my lungs and records the pressure of my blood.

"When was her last cycle?"

Ryker clears his throat. "She's been here for ten days. Nothing in that time." His voice is low and gruff.

The doctor merely nods and presses a needle into a bottle, drawing the liquid into the syringe.

When he goes to inject it into my arm, I jerk away. "What is it?"

The doctor doesn't answer and instead wraps his fingers around my upper arm, holding tightly and pulling me back toward him. I tense, resisting his grasp and the doctor turns to Ryker.

"Hold her still, would you?"

It is only then that Ryker actually looks at me. His eyes lift slowly, and I'm once more struck by the torment they hold. Dark clouds are gathering in their depths, but I don't know what they mean. He swallows once and turns his gaze to the doctor.

"What is it?" he asks.

Letting go of my arm, the doctor passes him a note. "My list of instructions," he says. "Now will you hold her?"

Ryker scans the note then nods and walks around to the head of my bed, lowering his hands to hold me in place. I try to move away but the pain stops me.

Tears prick my eyes. "I just want to know what it is."

Ryker shakes his head, but when his fingers wrap around my arm to pull it toward the doctor, his touch his gentle. Almost apologetic. The needle pierces my skin and the liquid is pushed into my flesh. I feel nothing but a cool sensation in my arm.

Placing everything back into his case, the doctor gets to his feet, his eyes falling over me as though I'm nothing more than a body on a table.

"She will be fine. It will take a while for everything to heal but as long as you regularly apply the cream, I don't anticipate any scarring or permanent damage. I will leave you with more painkillers and some cream and some bandages to attend to her. But I would suggest you use a less aggressive method for submission in the future."

I expect Ryker to protest at the doctor's words and insist that it wasn't him who inflicted this, but Ryker merely nods and follows the doctor toward the door.

"Ryker?" I say, my voice barely a whisper.

He stops for a moment, but his back is to me and he doesn't turn.

"Ryker, please look at me."

My words get caught in the base of my throat, as though Marcel's fingers are still there and trying to stop them from escaping. There's a slump to Ryker's shoulders that I haven't seen before, but he still doesn't turn.

And I've never felt so alone as when he walks out that door. I want to beg for him to come back. If I could handle the pain, I would kneel before the camera in perfect submission and hope he saw. Anything just to make him come back. Anything to feel the safety of him. Because if he is here, Marcel can't hurt me.

No one can.

Except for him.

He gets stuck in my mind and I can't escape him. I wonder who he must be outside these walls, if he has people that care about him, a person who is waiting for him to come home. I wonder about his childhood and what sort of life he must have had that has made him forget. From the hesitation in the way he treats me, I know he is battling something within. Something that torments him.

When the painkiller begins to work and I find a few moments of sleep, it's Ryker's face that haunts my dreams. But in them we aren't trapped in a cell. We are free. We are together. And we are happy. And when I wake, I'm not sure which hurts more. The pulsing thud of pain dulled slightly by the pills, or the realization that my dream will never be true.

But when the hushed hiss of air enters the room with the opening of the door hours later, it isn't Ryker who appears. It's Star. My heart starts pounding, scared that Marcel will follow, but the door eases shut behind her and I let out a sob of relief.

She doesn't look at me as she walks over to the bed, tray

in hand, her eyes trained obediently to the ground even though it is just the two of us. She's dressed in a night slip like I am. Like I was, before Marcel tore it from my body.

I'm trembling under the blanket. Ever since his attack, I can't seem to get warm. The room is kept cool at all times, but my body had become accustomed to it, regulating itself to adjust. Now, it is as though the cold has seeped into my bones, although my skin is on fire.

Star kneels beside the bed, lowering the tray to the ground. "I've brought you some food." Her voice is soft and gentle, barely a whisper. "And some cream for your wounds." She still doesn't look at me. I want her to. I need her to.

"Star." It feels like years since I've spoken. My voice is broken and torn. The bruises around my throat make it hurt. "Star," I say again, begging her to look at me. I need someone to remind me that I'm still here.

The bruises on her sides have faded to yellowish-brown. Remnants of black circle her eye. The left side of her upper lip is still slightly swollen, but the cut is healed, clean from blood.

She plays with the food on the tray, rearranging it so none of the fruit touches. "Are you hungry?" she asks. And then she lifts eyes so pale it's as if they have no color at all, and they lock on mine. There is nothing behind them. No emotion. No desperation or fear. Nothing but acceptance.

A sob lodges itself at the back of my throat. I cannot become like her. She's given up. Accepted her fate.

"You should eat." Gingerly, she picks up a slice of apple and holds it out to me. It hovers in front of my mouth, waiting for me to open. All the fruit has already been sliced. Ryker usually brings a knife. My dreams have often been stuck on it.

I'm lying on the bed, resting on my side, unable or unwilling to move. I don't open my mouth but stare into her eyes, searching for the girl who must be in there.

"Eat whenever they offer food. You don't know when it's next coming."

Except, I did. Ryker appeared with food three times a day. But from the way Star's skin was stretched over her bones, I knew it wasn't the same for her.

Slowly I open my mouth and she pops in the slice of apple. My jaw aches when I chew, and the sweetness starts gurgles of nausea in my gut.

"Eat," she says. It's not a command. It's a request. A plea.

I chew and swallow, tears smarting as the apple slides down my throat.

"You've got to keep up your strength," she says. "There's no place for stubbornness here. It will get you nowhere."

I swallow the last of the apple and open my mouth again when she offers another slice. I'm not sure why she's feeding me, but there's something comforting about it. Reminds me of Mum.

"How long have you been here?" I whisper.

She looks at the camera. The red light is on. But for some

reason, she answers. She leans forward, so close that her breath hits me as she speaks.

"I don't know. It's a while." Her voice lowers even more, something I didn't think possible and I have to strain to hear her. "No one wants me," she says.

There is sadness there, as though she wants to be sold.

"You haven't been requested?" I ask.

She shakes her head, holding out another slice of apple. There is a hint of jealousy to the set of her jaw.

"How many girls do they have here?"

She shrugs. "It's hard to tell."

I become desperate for information, firing questions at her as quickly as they form in my head.

"Do you know where we are? Do you know who runs this place, any of the names other than Marcel? How did you get here?"

But she ignores my questions, picking up another piece of apple and playing with it between her fingers, seemingly becoming transfixed with the redness of its flesh.

I sigh, knowing my questions will go unanswered. "You can eat it if you like."

Without hesitation, she pops it into her mouth, and it's the first time I've seen any emotion from her. Pure bliss.

"I was larger when I came here," she explains. "Marcel controlled my food in order to help me lose the weight." There's no malice in her voice, in fact, it's almost as though she's grateful. "Maybe next auction I will be sold. Maybe it will be to someone kind."

I swallow my repulsion. "Does he hit you often?"

She shakes her head. "Only when I need it."

"When you need it?" I just about choke.

She nods, picking up another slice of apple and offering it to me. I shake my head and she puts it into her mouth without prompting.

"It took a while for me to learn to behave." She smiles sadly. "Don't be like me. This will happen time and time again unless you learn to obey." The apple seems to have given her energy. She smiles, her movements are less stilted. "Roll onto your stomach. I'll put cream on those wounds."

I do as she requests and brace myself for the feel of her fingers on my broken skin. The cream is cold, but she is gentle. Once she's done, she leans in close.

"What did you do? Why isn't he doing this?"

"What do you mean?"

"Marcel is always the one to look after me when I'm in pain. He's always the one to soothe my wounds. You must have done something really bad if they are making me do it instead."

"It wasn't Ryker who did this to me." I move my head so I'm looking directly at her. "It was Marcel."

Her hand stills on my back. "Marcel?" There is a hint of pain in her voice. "Marcel did this to you?" Her eyes well with tears.

I nod, watching her closely. She's upset.

She swallows, her eyes falling to the ground. "Did he touch you in other ways too?"

With her words the feel of his erection pressing against me, his fingers inside me, come flooding back. A slick cold sweat covers my body and my heart starts to pound, the rush of blood deafening. I draw in a deep breath and let it out slowly. When I open my eyes again, she's staring directly at me, waiting for my reply. And that's when it occurs to me. She loves him.

So I shake my head, wanting to spare this girl any pain I can. "I wouldn't obey. He was punishing me for disobedience."

She smiles.

It breaks my heart.

Gathering a towel from the tray, she wipes her hands clean, gathers everything she brought with her and gets to her feet. "The cream will help." Walking toward the door, she pushes it open, then looks back at me. "Next time," she says, "just submit."

"Star?" Her eyes narrow a little when I use her name again. Or, what I assume is her name. She hasn't told me any differently. "Have you seen him?"

She frowns, and her lips pinch together, turning them white. "Marcel?"

I shake my head. "Ryker."

"He's the one who sent me in here to look after you."

I shuffle up on the bed, propping myself up on my

elbows. "So, you've seen him?"

And that's when I hear it. The eagerness in my voice, the desperation to hear about him.

Star's frown flattens. Her head tilts to one side but she doesn't need to say anything. It's all there in her expression.

I'm just like her.

BOOKS BY SABRE ROSE

Thornton Brothers

(Contemporary Romance Series)

Touched

Tempted

Taken

Torn

Tears

You Ruined Me

(A Tragic Dark Romance Novella)

Requested Trilogy

(Dark Romance Series)

Don't Say A Word

Until You're Mine

My Sweet Songbird

Made in the USA
Lexington, KY
02 May 2019